Afterlife

Afterlife

Angela Woodward

FC2
TUSCALOOSA

Copyright © 2026 by Angela Woodward

The University of Alabama Press

Tuscaloosa, Alabama 35487-0380

All rights reserved

FC2 is an imprint of the University of Alabama Press

Inquiries about reproducing material from this work should be addressed to the University of Alabama Press

Book Design: Publications Unit, Department of English, Illinois State University; Director: Steve Halle, Production Assistant: Tate Lewis-Carroll
Cover design: Matthew Revert
Typeface: Adobe Jenson Pro

Library of Congress Cataloging-in-Publication Data is available from the Library of Congress.

Paper: 978-1-57366-216-1
Ebook: 978-1-57366-919-1

Contents

1 □ Afterlife
3 □ Birds in Art
5 □ BUtterfield 8
7 □ Cadmium
11 □ Conformity
14 □ Cults
18 □ Dark
21 □ David Copperfield
24 □ Elton John
28 □ Encyclopedias
36 □ Fallujah
39 □ Future
43 □ Gloria
49 □ History
52 □ Horses
57 □ Insects
60 □ Invasion of the Body Snatchers
63 □ Jest
69 □ Klaprothium
72 □ Labor

77 □	Love
80 □	Michigan
84 □	Motion
89 □	Names
92 □	Numinous
99 □	Occult
102 □	Poets
106 □	Quiet
108 □	Rye Crackers
111 □	Struck
117 □	Trusted Source
122 □	Umbrellas
128 □	Voorhees
132 □	Waiting
135 □	Waste
140 □	Xyz
143 □	Acknowledgments

Afterlife

For weeks I've been having troubling visions of my demise. I don't preview my death from asphyxiation or a car crash or a dread disease, but while sleeping I encounter a heightened state I recognize as not belonging to this life. I'm surrounded by friends and family, moving with unity and purpose.

I lined all my lovers up and ranked them from my first to my present one, and the man who found himself my favorite out of all of them came with me to a hotel. At last I was in his arms again, smelling his hair, hearing him speak to a passerby in the hallway. A whole group of children came with us, orphans, asking for adult guidance in playing soccer. They wanted to improve their skills. What are his credentials? their coach asked me. Couldn't be better, I said. You can look him up. The whiny, recalcitrant, angry and unfocused boys followed my lover's directions. He revealed the secrets of the game to them. They felt unified, their whole bodies flowing into their running feet instead of their heads floating above, disconnected in their clouds of blame.

I traveled to a foreign city to give a concert of music I'd composed. When I stood at the podium, I realized I'd forgotten my score. It was on my bed, back at the hotel. I could only get to the hotel by crossing a bridge that was so steep, I had to pull myself along, grabbing the railings, to get past the height of its arc. In spite of this obstacle, which would be just as difficult on the return trip, I thought I'd be gone just a few minutes. I found my father at the hotel waiting for me, all dressed up in a brown suit. But you're dead, I said. There's no need to come to my concert. It will be too hard for you.

He very much wanted to be there, he said. He was all ready to come. I wondered how I was going to get this dear old man back over that suspension bridge which I, in all my youth and strength, had barely made it over.

My sister sat down on my bed. But Vicky, I said, you died just three weeks ago. What are you doing here? She shrugged. She was always a fuck-up, she implied. Even when she had passed away, she couldn't make it stick, but kept hanging around. I was glad that she said this with a look and a gesture, and didn't shout or snarl at me, like on many other occasions. In the afterlife my constant humiliating of her, and her of me, had mutated into something fizzy and stinging, like ginger ale.

Birds in Art

A MUSEUM IN WISCONSIN DISPLAYS NOTHING but paintings of birds, except sculptures of birds—the pigeon, the duck, the crow, the ostrich, the gull, the sparrow, sometimes in close-up, sometimes just a smudge against the scenery. The person who began the museum died long ago, but her fortune lives on. The museum's foundation bestows a trip to central Wisconsin on painters and sculptors from Nova Scotia, Japan, and even New Zealand for the annual gala. Many men and women come to see the paintings of birds, and on the opening night they mingle with the creators of these bird images.

What wonderful birds they are, some drawn in loving realism, some scrawled in charcoal or carved out of their own feathers, little black birds on white sticks that are the skeletons of the devices that had set them free. Relatively few people are depicted with the birds, though there are a couple hunters, shown from the back. The visitor moving from room to room can't keep her eyes from meeting the little round eyes of the birds. The visitor might get sick of their importuning within twenty minutes.

In a gallery beyond the new paintings of birds hang several older, gold-framed paintings of dead birds hung by their feet.

These paintings are calming not only because the birds aren't staring, but because they call up if not flat out belong to a school of art: the still life. The way they're arranged on the canvas head down, these dead birds put the visitor in mind of the Dutch masters with their jugs and vegetables, meals without people, implements without any hands holding them. The painters of the dead birds had hewn to a tradition, while the painters of swallows and sparrows in flight might have sat themselves down to paint birds for reasons of their own that had nothing to do with what anyone else considered art-worthy. This seems so lonely, even if on the other side of the world, a woman had decided to collect only paintings of birds.

BUtterfield 8

THE WRITERS OF ONE HUNDRED YEARS AGO WAILED against conformity. They felt that one person was expected to live their life much like another person, and this was wrong. The steps a person took to make themselves less like other people were punished by other people. The woman who indulged her sexual cravings, married or not, and the man who cursed the United States and his father-in-law's chemical factory, came to bad ends, these writers demonstrated. Before the crack-up came light, suffering, and the truth.

In *BUtterfield 8*, the novelist John O'Hara takes a few pages to detail the happenings around the town: "James J. Walker, mayor of the city of New York, had a late lunch at the Hardware Club. A girl using an old curling iron caused a short circuit in the Pan-Hellenic Club." The buzz of the big city, always event, is circumscribed into tribal contexts. Here are only two sentences, but O'Hara pads out half a chapter with it. He may have expected us to take it all in, marveling at his eye for the mundane. But surely that's not what happens. His reader brushes by this section, skimming ahead to land on the promiscuous woman Gloria's revelation about why she's so bad.

The writers of one hundred years ago felt they had to make definite moral statements. John O'Hara sat at his desk, itching for a whiskey. It would be so much easier to be one of the souses he wrote about, golden youths destroying their gifts with drink and abandon while their parents and neighbors trundled along with their small talk and doctor's appointments. Yet it was he who was trapped in a straightjacket of habits, doling out his prose day after day, words like two-by-fours, sentences like train cars, paragraphs like the false fronts of small-town dime stores.

Cadmium

CADMIUM EXHIBITS WONDERFUL PROPERTIES as a pigment. It produces colors from lemon yellow to the yellow-orange of a mango to the brilliant red of stoplights. It can be heated to a high degree without flaking or blistering. While portrait painters daubed tiny patches of cadmium yellow to light up the floral background behind a lady's head, factory workers sprayed cadmium paints directly out of grimy nozzles onto steam pipes and machine parts. Cadmium has no known biological function in higher organisms. It is not used as a dietary supplement. Healers don't grind it into almond paste and serve it to women who feel that they must improve their base nature. Cadmium paints have long-lasting properties and can be applied to glass, and to metal parts subjected to heat and stress. The red stars that adorn the Kremlin gain their color from cadmium. These, lit up at night and in the gloomy afternoon, shine their beacons undisturbed. Their red doesn't fade with time, or not in the amount of time a human being notices.

The United States Army sprayed zinc cadmium sulfide over Minneapolis in 1950. The United States Army declared in its own records that this substance *was not known* to cause health problems if inhaled or ingested. This is at least a misstatement, if not a knowing falsehood. The zinc cadmium sulfide was employed as a simulant. Its actions in the air mimicked another substance, maybe plutonium, that was actually malicious. The cadmium wafted out of blowers and sifted onto window ledges, over roof tops, onto parking lots. It clung to the eaves of doghouses and coated the chilly slats of park benches. A woman walked to the corner store, holding her hat onto her head with one hand, and with the other leading a reluctant little boy. "I don't want to walk!" he said. "You're big enough now," she answered. He'd spent the past week lying on his back with his feet in the air, sucking his thumb. He was playing his version of his baby self, this younger him who he felt had a better deal than his current form. The substance burrowed into the felt of his mother's hat. The little boy drew it into his lungs as he pulled against his mother's grip on his wrist. "Danny, don't," she said.

The cadmium swirled up and around corners, tossed by the whims of that shiftless joker, the wind. The wind in Minneapolis blows primarily on the napes of its inhabitants, following them and easing itself into the patches of skin exposed above the shirt collar. Even on the coldest days, many of the inhabitants wear only a plaid shirt and rationalize that they don't have far to go. I've seen Minneapolis residents walking to work in gym shorts in February, bare legs sticking out of an unzipped puffy coat. Women run to the bus stop in high-heeled sandals, not even bothering to pull their gloves out of their pockets. The wind keeps up a steady huff against the backs of these people's necks and bare knees and exposed wrists.

Eighty-one field experiment hours and eleven thousand, one hundred and seventy man-hours went into the diffusion of zinc cadmium sulfide over Minneapolis in 1950. Crews of men sent out the substance with foggers or blowers at various points around the city. From street corners and from the balconies of three-story boarding houses, they set the simulant loose. They had contacted the city government and said that they would be studying ways to shroud a city in smoke to hide it in case of nuclear attack. Some cities were being considered to take part in this experiment, and it was possible that Minneapolis was one of them. If something were to happen, or seem to happen, this shrouding experiment might be what had taken place. That was all they could say. Residents were not to be informed, but the city government received this smidgen of information about a tentative operation. The notes I was able to acquire through a publicly available source reveal that the parks commissioner objected, though none of his words are recorded. The notes say only that this problem was solved when the role of parks commissioner changed hands during a new city administration. He could have been fired, or left in outrage, after his demands for more information about this operation went unanswered. He could have been one of those people who started the trend to move to Montana in search of freedom. His friends probably called him a crank. He should have retired long ago, they said behind his back. After all, he'd been too old to fight overseas. All the young men coming back and getting married needed jobs like his.

Cadmium may enter the body by ingestion or inhalation, entry by inhalation representing the greater hazard. In France, three hundred workers who had drunk wine kept in cadmium-lined containers became ill, some seriously. Symptoms included weakness and gastrointestinal distress. Other workers were diagnosed with cadmium poisoning from inhalation after they had melted cadmium ingots in a poorly ventilated room. They reported dryness of the throat, headache, nausea and brown urine. Symptoms of chronic cadmium poisoning among workers making ferro-nickel storage batteries were preceded by a characteristic yellow pigmentation of the teeth. This is known as the "yellow ring of cadmium."

A doctor described the case of a worker who succumbed to thick yellow fumes given off when cutting up cadmium-plated steel torpedo heads. Another worker died five days after shaking by hand molten metal containing 10 percent cadmium. Six similar cases had been seen over eight years, all exhibiting the same symptoms of weakness, chronic bronchitis, and loss of weight.

An industrial iron, such as those used to smooth cloth in textile factories, may be coated with a cadmium pigment due to its excellent heat resistance. School buses, known for their brilliant yellow, in fact owe their hue to cadmium. Anyone who has lived on a county highway has encountered the piercing glare of school bus headlights, accompanied by a rotating orange beam in the middle of the roof. Out of the fog the bus itself finally arrives, publishing its ghastly hue. Anyone who has rented a shitty little house up a road from a county highway knows the persistence of fog in its ditches, and the waist-high billowings on practically any morning. The school bus wades through the dense vapor, its wheels invisible but its yellow sides appearing in segments. The windows are black in the early morning. The school kids lean their heads against them and listen to music through their earbuds, oblivious, half conscious, or all the way asleep.

Conformity

No one is interested in conformity any more. The writers of one hundred years ago made it their main subject, but their readers have moved on. Conformity doesn't seem to be the problem that men and women must break the bonds of, the expectations of parents, the rules of dress and behavior, the ban on loving fully and erotically instead of indulging fondness long enough so that it leads to the birth of several children. The novelists of today have given up on it as a subject.

John O'Hara was perhaps the last to scratch the mirrored surface of American conformity and find there a whispering mist shaping writhing forms. Oh, the despair of eating at the country club once again! O'Hara's protagonist in BUtterfield 8 fills an afternoon with his wife and children and various friends in the club's restaurant. A Black man takes his order, asking, "What about some veg'ables?" The chemical company executive waves his hand and instructs, "Just bring us a lot of vegetables." Needless to say, this waiter is never heard from again. Various dark-skinned servants amble through BUtterfield 8 in near silence. They are not depicted as quasi animals, leading a life of sensual fulfillment denied to their wealthy white compatriots. In fact there's a slight prickle, as instances of distaste for these servants and elevator operators is probed, character to character, as if with the longing to be free of the infinite boredom of matrimony comes a sense of . . . a scent on the air like . . . charcoal? . . . injustice. Someone knows something is not right here. The board tilts. These men who groan at being wealthy and proper have a glimmer of understanding, that not only are they suffering, they are causing suffering. Not that they'll do much about it.

The story of the waiter paints itself in reverse, how he too is caught in a pattern not of his own making. The freedom he longs for is simply to walk down the street after sundown without fear of being jumped by the teenage sons of the yearning chemical company executive. He enjoys the moon reflected in the swimming pool as much as any of the country club members, more really, since the towel draped over his arm also partakes of the shimmer after midnight. The dishcloth magnifies, now center of the scene, while the man's face recedes.

The chemical company executive, Weston Liggett, has met Gloria, a beautiful socialite, a heavy drinker who's said to have slept with all of Yale. He's ripped her dress down the front to get her out of it, a moment neither of them can stop thinking about.

Liggett calls *love* what's clearly ruin. He hounds Gloria to her death. Conformity for her might mean loving the children she would have, if she were the kind of woman the kind of man Liggett is would marry. She would vow to treat her kids better than she had been. This was not hard to do, since her widowed mother had pointedly left her alone with a family friend who paid their rent. It's generous of O'Hara to realize that his character had been bought and sold since she was six years old, and her sexual indulgences are a way of trying to take control of the account books

herself. She's her own CEO of mayhem and hangover. It would be so much better if Gloria would fall for some floozy, perhaps her friend Steve's adventurous girlfriend Norma, and the two of them could turn their back on the whole clothes-money-sex thing. On their farm upstate. As if
    that
    was
    the way out.
    Invasion of the Body Snatchers?

Cults

MANY CULTS DON'T HAVE NAMES, and the people in them don't even know they're in a cult. It's just something they're doing with some other people, a way of living, in a farmhouse or at a campground, with a set of goals. People talk about the *cult following* of their local football team. They mock their coworkers as *blind cultists* for endorsing the newly introduced policies of one of the regional managers. Meanwhile, a woman who quit her job, left her latest boyfriend, and moved across the country to an undisclosed location with five people she met at a lecture has no idea she's in a cult. This woman might just think she's finally fitting in and enjoying herself. When she doesn't call but sends only the rare odd postcard, this woman's mother and stepdad say to each other, "She's joined a cult." Only after the woman manages to extricate herself will she slowly begin to fit the word *cult* onto the years spent, mostly happily, with the leader and all the others.

Because a cult is defined primarily retroactively, at the time when those who have left reflect on their experience, it's useful to have a method to determine what constitutes a cult in the present moment. Cult leaders and their followers can be distinguished by a particular light, rootless laugh. It's a brief chuckle that interrupts speech, and occurs mostly when the tenets of the non-cult world must be shown to be useless, if not actually harmful. The words for laughter include *giggle, chuckle, titter, guffaw, snort, snicker, snigger, chortle*—most of which should never be used in writing or in conversation—plus various sounds used as shorthand such as *ha ha, hee hee, he he*. These too are just about useless. Maybe what's most important about this particular cult laugh is that it invokes a response. When the leader inserts this hollow, mirthless laugh into their speech, the followers immediately chime in with their own version of it. This interpolated titter is a way of soliciting agreement.

When everyone is smoothly interlocked into the cult's thinking, certain words evoke the laugh—like *evil, bodies, lust, money, ambition*. All anyone has to say is, "You know, *love* ..." with a pause, and the cult members laugh the cult laugh. They titter the cult titter. Something these people formerly wrecked their lives over—searching for a partner, slapping the face of the man they used to adore when he tenderly touched their arm, crying all night about the equally ugly alternatives of leaving this lover or staying with him—have now dissolved into the dust of this brief chuckle. It's a dry laugh without a source in the belly, a kind of nasal, monotone, unmelodic couple of syllables. Meaning, all *that* is over. Who cares? It's a laugh without empathy, and signally, without humor. The emotion conjured is closer to pity, with a bit of fondness, like for a sick pet snake before dad takes it out to the bushes to "recover." The child's feelings for the animal are not included in this laugh. Only the adult's understanding that something has to be done, and unfortunately, dad is the one to do it. There's tedium in this laugh. People and their problems are so boring, this chuckle implies. This laugh resembles a tumbleweed, the skeletal structure of all that formerly would have made the cultists spring with joy or sorrow now desiccated. The cult leader's laugh, and the laugh of his followers, set up their own ghost town of abandoned mines and emptied warehouses. There's no one left to *care* in this place. And isn't that just great? this polite *ha ha* manages to get across. We've finally left all *that*.

I met a woman at a place I rented briefly in California, a boarding house where about a hundred women lived together in cheap little rooms with a bathroom in the hall. Not a cult. Just a large building, where any woman was free to come and go, to rent, sublet, flee in the night, or stay for years. Every evening, this woman hung around by the pay phone. Not right in front of it, but near enough so that if it rang, she would be the one to answer it. She was from China. She had met her husband when he traveled to China on business. He worked in computers. He had promised her money, security and education if she married him and came away to California. He hadn't told her that back in the States he lived in a compound with many other couples and families, and that once back there, they would not be permitted to travel. His paycheck went into a communal fund. She couldn't go to a grocery store or a movie. Every evening the group had talks, she said, usually grilling someone's faults. The faults were often hers. She had been punished by having her hair cut, time after time.

Her hair was still quite short, though she'd been letting it grow ever since she left that gated community where her husband lived. She wasn't getting a divorce, she stressed. It wasn't him but that *place* she had left. She couldn't stand living with all those others and being constantly scolded. Her husband had given her some cash and helped her get to Oakland. He told her he would follow in a few weeks. She held out the likelihood, every evening, that he would call her.

Her husband, still in the cult, probably didn't experience the indigo slant of those hours spent near the pay phone, waiting. It wasn't all sad. She, the one who broke away, had found our little group of women from China, Thailand, South Korea, and Michigan, separately cooking pots of rice, frying vegetables, and discussing our backgrounds, hopes, and the ridiculous fake eyelashes of the assistant manager of the boarding house. The assistant manager aspired to be a Mary Kay beauty consultant, and dressed like a six-foot baby-blue baby doll. If you locked yourself out of your room, she was the one you had to ask for the master key. She could have been nicer about it.

People who are vulnerable to being exploited by cults are often seekers. They're looking for something. This is a dangerous state, this desire to fill an emptiness. And yet it's people who are satisfied who are the most distressing. As if nothing is wrong, they've got it all figured out. People like that are unbearable.

Dark

THIS IS HOW THE ENGLISH novelist Elizabeth Taylor describes the evening descending over a small seaside town in *A View of the Harbour*: "In winter the dusk settles down over the earth like a fine powder, solidifying, making the air opaque, until houses are buried in it, mounded over as if with snow, and all the pastel colours deepen into darkness."

She gives the darkness palpability. She describes it without reference to that shiny loudmouth, light. The dark is not a quality of sight either, but a material force accumulating. It piles up over blues and pinks until they're covered with it, and altered. The dark is tactile, with a heaviness, gravity. The features of the evening town stand up merely as indicators of the particularities of darkness, as if the whole place were nothing but a complex meter for apprehending this alien precipitate.

I ran into a woman named Helen at the apartment of my friend Tia. Helen told me how she'd done a small workshop and reading with the professors of the little college in Janesville where she had a temporary position a few years back. She had signed up to do a faculty research sharing event, she told me, at the little college where she taught two Intro to Lit classes. The submission form had made clear that "creative output" would also be appropriate for this faculty workshop, and she found herself at a round table of seven guests all ostensibly signed up to hear her speak about her poetry. She started out, she told me, explaining that the material she was about to read was "dark," and might be upsetting. Instantly a man at the table asked her to stop and reconsider her choice of words. She wanted to say, he said, that her poem dealt with emotionally or politically charged or turbulent material. It might be troubling, or dig up strong emotions. But to say that it was "dark" meant it was bad, sad, or dangerous, qualities that had clung to him his whole life due only to the color of his skin. "Let me stop you right there and have you consider," he said.

"Thank you, I will," she said. And now she was completely tongue-tied. All the words she had rehearsed had to do with darkness, with approaching the dark, with dredging up dark events, with daring to shine a light into dark places of the psyche and the political beast. She was writing about the rape of a female soldier, something a friend of hers had heard from a friend of hers. The poem was set in a closet, an unlit storage space within a dim hallway within a gray industrial building. She wondered if she could read something else, but it was all about the same, she thought— one gigantic metaphor of dark meaning bad.

"So how did you continue your workshop?" I asked. "Were you angry at him for stopping you?"

She wasn't, she said. It was a confusing situation for her, but she was glad he'd spoken up. If it hadn't been for that intimate setting, the eight of them at the round table, the lone Black man in attendance might not have felt comfortable saying what he thought. She needed to hear his objection, and take it into account. The problem was that she was forced to see her whole opus differently, within the span of a couple of seconds. Not only her planned presentation and the poem about the rape of the soldier, but many other pieces of prose and poetry she was proud of now appeared to her completely lacking in insight into the language they were built out of. Her poem was meant to make a story of brutality unfold for its listeners as a series of felt moments. The cold of the door handle. The silence of the brooms and mops. Voices in a neighboring hallway. She had wanted to create a version of the rape she'd been told about that emptied it of some feelings and poured others in, though in its aftereffect the listener would remember their original feelings, the perhaps unexamined ones, and find them altered. Her poem, she said, was meant to be a little machine for transformation, which would for a moment alleviate the horror of the attack it described and then create a cloud of a different responsibility for it.

"All that went to shit," she said. "Everything I'd ever written seemed totally stupid. Like I could transform anything at all, using this unsuitable instrument, the English language."

"Wow," I said. Tia looked at her lap, then at the clock above the stove. It was really hard to find anything appropriate to say, we must have both thought. I coughed, like my bronchitis was acting up. Tia hopped up to boil more water for tea. Did we want cookies? she asked, and opened a couple drawers looking for them. She fussed around arranging a plate of four stale lemon cremes for the three of us.

I thought I might run into this poet Helen another time, but she was moving out of town. In fact she'd only be here another week. "Give me your email then," I said. She dutifully wrote it down on a little piece of paper for me.

David Copperfield

ONE HUNDRED YEARS BEFORE THE UNITED STATES Army diffused zinc cadmium sulfide over it in a secret and mostly unremarked operation, the city of Minneapolis had been only a collection of shacks in the shadow of a fort. Settlers searched through Fort Snelling's garbage dump for suitable lumber and nailed together soap boxes and bark to make rough shelters. The captain of the fort had on several occasions driven the settlers away by ripping the roofs off their abodes. No one would have called these contraptions "houses," and that word is never used in my sources for the history of Minneapolis. Nevertheless, men persisted in traveling to the area around Fort Snelling in the hopes that a change in the government would allow them to buy land. Until then, they occupied small plots, winding twine around sticks stuck in their putative property's corners.

Game of every kind ambled through the area's forests and fields. Raccoons, wildcats, gray wolves, foxes, deer, and game birds such as prairie hen, partridge, and pigeons made a nuisance of themselves at the edges of the settlement. This abundance was met by an utter lack of game laws. Nothing prevented men with guns from taking out anything that moved. Huntsmen arrived in droves in the early autumn, renting out all the sheds and lean-tos the settlers could spare. These gentlemen invaded the town from many parts of the world, speaking German, Russian, French, and Swedish. The settlers woke their guests before dawn and paraded them out to the untamed countryside. At the end of the day, carts laden with carcasses blocked the spaces between the shacks, and blood leaked into the dirt passageways.

Despite how roughly the settlers lived, they adored mental refinements. One October, a man arrived with a copy of *David Copperfield*. Dickens's novel had just been published, and the volume in the settler's luggage might have been the only one in the whole Minnesota Territory. The book's owner turned its pages under the blue sky as well as in the flickering, noxious tallow light of his hut after dinner. The other settlers watched him walk into the woods, book in hand. They had not glimpsed some of its scenes in one of many movie adaptations while idly flipping through channels on a lonely weekend. Their older sister hadn't been assigned the book in her Advanced Placement British Lit class. They had not acted out an extremely condensed version of it in a children's after-school theater class. *David Copperfield*'s story at that time was altogether unfamiliar.

The book's original owner passed it to his neighbor when he finished it. This man too spent hours enraptured, moving his eyes over lines of print at any interval between tasks. Then he gave it to the man next door. Some of the settlers had little to do once they'd skinned a few rabbits, and for them, young David Copperfield's life flew by. Dickens's hero was educated, abandoned, rescued, married, and then remarried over the course of a couple weeks. Over the duration of one snowstorm, David discovered the goodness in people, and gave up his bitter resentment. In the hands of the next reader, David watched small donkeys trip-trap past his great-aunt Betsey's house, while in the woods, curious yellow flowers poked their snouts out of naked leaf duff. Young David, on his own in London, washed bottles in a dingy warehouse and wandered the city to watch coal-heavers dancing on the wharf. By the time summer arrived in the territory, with its birdsong and stifling heat, all the settlers had read *David Copperfield*, and the volume was worn to tatters.

Elton John

I stopped thinking about my sister Vicky after the first couple months or so. Lots of people died around the time she died, including famous jazz drummers and painters and the elderly mother of a dear friend. It wasn't unusual to know someone who had died, or to be a person trying to go on without someone who had died, and I did a pretty terrible job of focusing on Vicky after her sudden decline. Recently, I had dinner with some friends, a rare occasion where Tia called a couple of us and we met at a place near where two of us live, on a weeknight. It was so nice. During the meal, we talked about our travels and the follies of the upper echelons of the administration at the various places we worked or used to work. Over the dirty plates, we talked about death and dying. The daughter of one of the foolish administrators we had maligned earlier had recently died in a traffic accident. Her car had flipped the barrier and headed the wrong way on an interior highway, one of those heavily traveled commuter paths that are the most dangerous stretches of road. It was unclear whether she had lost consciousness before losing control of the car—it could have been epilepsy or a drug overdose that led to the crash. The toxicology report would take months, and in the meantime, this administrator had been prevented from claiming his daughter's body.

Strangely, this same administrator's assistant had almost died, and was either recovering slowly or gradually coming to terms with the fact that she wouldn't make it. She was on extended medical leave. One of our friends had visited her in the hospital. She was so weak, our friend said, that she couldn't pull the covers up over herself on the bed. She lay there shivering, unable to lift her hand and push the call button for the nurse. Speaking slowly, she explained that she was simply very tired, our friend told us.

Long before my sister died, she'd written a book of poems. That is, for a period of about two months, Vicky had written a poem or two every day, and after her death our eldest sister Althea had collected them into a spiral-bound booklet. We may have read a poem or two, years ago, at the time Vicky was writing them. Doubtless we said, *oh great, nice job,* or something completely noncommittal. It wouldn't be like either of us to praise something that was in fact just the sketchiest observation made into a poem by line breaks. Rain. The wind. Althea and I were the kind of people who would be politely uninterested in poems that made as if to record the passage of a cat across a rug, Althea because she's a scientist, and me because I'm an artist. Most of Vicky's poems read like slightly sad greeting cards, with exceedingly commonplace sentiments. It's no surprise to find that in one of them, she describes the moon as

> *like an*
> *ancient*
> *silver coin*

the effect being more like a version of something she'd read than any acute observation or the capturing of a moment of personal intensity.

While I taught myself slowly and not too well to play the piano, Vicky said that she would like to be a genius, like Elton John. Elton John, she told me, had sat down at the piano as a child and was immediately able to play anything he heard. Not like me, she meant. My older sister simultaneously disdained my efforts and aspired to an almost magical ability with the instrument for herself. She just hadn't sat down yet, to find out if she had Elton John's talent. One day we would know. I continued to fumble through my simple Bach and Haydn, while also continuing to feel discouraged by Vicky's remark.

It was just as easy to wound her, a perpetual outcast. I didn't refrain from it at any point, adulthood failing to call a truce on childhood's bitter battle. Vicky seems to have died from the same illness that attacked the assistant of the administrator at my friend's workplace. Vicky lost the ability to move, and finally to breathe, through no known cause. Her illness was given a name that meant "it's not all these other things it could be, all the similar diseases that immediately spring to mind when you hear of someone without the strength to lift even a piece of toast."

Vicky hadn't dealt with her mysteriously progressing condition at all, until one day she called 9-1-1. The ambulance took her away while her neighbor was at work. This neighbor later said that she had knocked at Vicky's door every day, and wondered if she should call the police. Maybe Vicky had gone on vacation, but she thought Vicky would have told her she was leaving. It was only after months had passed, when Althea and I came to clear the apartment, that this neighbor learned what had happened.

"She used to knock at my door in a particular way," the neighbor told us, imitating the rhythm on the coffee table. Vicky often came by and sat in a chair in this neighbor's living room, as long as this neighbor didn't have her mother with her. One time recently, she had heard the knock. "Oh, Vicky's back," the neighbor said to herself. But when she opened the door, the outer hallway was empty. She was absolutely sure it had been Vicky's distinctive rapping. The neighbor tried to remember the date this happened. Could it have been the morning that Vicky died?

Althea and I consulted the calendars on our phones. We knew this neighbor would love to have received a spectral visit from our sister on her way to the other side. She had had a closeness with and fondness for Vicky that Althea and I didn't share. Our interactions with our sister had been much more complex than hers, or perhaps poisoned by our long history.

The neighbor waited, tensely smiling, while we two strangers opened apps and swiped left and right. But clearly, Althea and I agreed, the day of the mysterious knock could not have been that day. Not the day Vicky died. The knock had happened on one of those other days, where the date reigned over its little space on the calendar's grid, no appointments, no holiday, a day that had entered with morning and frayed into dusk but that still bore its numeral in case anyone came back to fill it with something in retrospect.

Encyclopedias

ENCYCLOPEDIAS CLOG BASEMENTS with their shelf-long bulk, the gold that gleamed so suavely in 1992 now embarrassingly dated, like the worst balding uncle at a bar mitzvah. Once, in all their splendor, every school had to have a set, and every upwardly aspiring household. Encyclopedias filled so much territory that whole cabinets were built to contain them, and rooms constructed to house the cabinets. Men and women were persuaded to fall in love and marry and have children only to turn out readers for encyclopedias. Whole generations were spawned simply to provide hands to turn the gilt-rimmed pages. The encyclopedia strives for wholeness and a universal classification system. The compiler's urge is to cover every possible topic—infinity categorized. The encyclopedia however doesn't escape its bounds, but like all of us takes up room, displaces water. Density where there might have been elasticity.

Pliny's work from 77 A.D., *Naturalis Historia*, treated even the shakiest sensory evidence with an air of authenticity. Both the known and the conjectured had equal weight. Pliny wrote at night, feverishly committing to the page summaries of others' letters and treatises, stories he had heard, and the numerous astonishments he himself had witnessed. He claimed to have seen personally a woman turn into a man at her wedding, and to have known a consul who never drank any liquid, on the advice of his doctor. He told of remote countries where the inhabitants had no noses. Beyond the noseless land were other lands where people had no upper lips, another where all were born without tongues, and another land where the people's lips were fused, and they could only eat what they could suck through a narrow oat straw. A certain man saw, along with all his attendants, a spark fall from the sky, grow as large as the moon, and then shrink down and become an ordinary lantern. Pliny's encyclopedia splayed out the world under precise headings: elephants, dragons, panthers, the river Ganges, medicines derived from human waste.

Everywhere travelers encountered forests, encyclopedias followed. Persian scholars observed the chill splendor of deciduous woodlands in the northern reaches of their empire. Each leaf had been written across by sun and wind, and now lay in shuffled heaps on the November ground. And so in the tenth century, the anonymous founders of the secret brotherhood the Brethren of Purity returned to Basra inspired to cover thousands of parchment pages with observations on cloud formations, insects, wool production, chastity, rope making, and sources of perfume. This scholarly work of the Muslim world set out in fifty-two volumes a mix of mathematics and parables, infused with mystic reverence for the number four. The Brethren of Purity's encyclopedia did not claim to be original or creative, but merely a compendium, a reflection, of all knowledge known. Similarly, the yellow wastes of beech forests modeled the *Prime Tortoise of the Record Bureau* for the intelligentsia of the Song dynasty in China. This series of volumes detailed types of harrow and many other agricultural topics, as well as battles of the past and royal genealogies. The *Prime Tortoise of the Record Bureau* distilled the jumble of past events and types of birds into a manageable system so that its aristocratic and bureaucratic readers would have a basis for making decisions. The encyclopedia sets itself up against *whim*.

Though Diderot is called a philosopher, he lived like many writers, scratching for any kind of work that might pay. His *Encyclopedie* (1751–1766) was in fact a freelance contract job, a translation of the English *Cyclopaedia* (1728) by Ephraim Chambers. Not content to reproduce the work, Diderot first aimed to shore it up with cutting-edge mathematics and then filled it with godless delusions. Diderot's *Encyclopedie* emphasized the work of hands and refused to treat religious topics. This meant that even a simple entry on haymaking took on heretical tones.

Scottish publishers struck back, coming out with a three-volume and then a twenty-volume *Encyclopedia Britannica* modeled on Diderot's but going bigger. Allegedly compiled by experts, and filled with stodgy sobriety, the new *Britannica* sold crisply. Commercial motives overshadowed all others as subsequent editions expanded its bulk. The Britannicists were unable to keep up with the demand for articles, and its editors cut and pasted freely from any available source. They doled debtors out of prison, then set them up to grind out copy. These indentured servants tried to earn back their freedom with "Shrimps," "Dust," "Moonlight," and "Hygiene." They knew little about anything, but laid down words and set up type. Or, they may have known quite a bit about things such as "Debtors' Prison," but turned in copy at deadline on royal lineages and chemical processes.

Consider the branching effect:
[diagram]

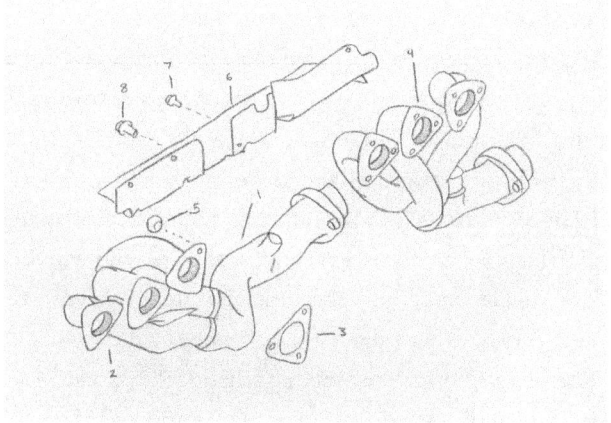

[image credit: Dave Buchen]

[caption: Anything included in an encyclopedia is given a badge of existence as well as a place in a grand scheme.]

[caption: In fact every fact is the same when burned to ash, the lives of saints, the invention of traffic signals, the uses of flax.]

[caption: A word that refers to the fitting of several pipes inside an internal combustion engine also means a whole that unites many diverse elements.]

[caption: Jets of soap blasted down on her car. A huge thing like a gate passed overhead. It looked from within the car like the car was moving, though she knew it was clamped into a boot on the carwash floor.]

The many volumes of the *Encyclopedia Britannica* produced those strangely suggestive half words, the spines stammering toward what they contained in phrases such as CHE—ECO and HUN—MOL. While the stiff binding and resplendent lettering proclaimed respectability, the publishers used all kinds of tricks, such as convincing readers to pay for the latest, newly updated edition though it was virtually the same as the old edition except for a few end notes. While many of the entries in *Britannica* were lifted from other sources without attribution, in the early twentieth century the Americans went one better and pirated the entire edition. At the time, no law prevented this. The Americans had a spy among the proofreaders, who sent back copy secretly. Another enterprising American used an early version of the Xerox copier to reproduce the *Britannica* and sell it under his own imprint.

In 1920, Sears, Roebuck bought out the original Scottish publishers of *Britannica*, and sweaty men hoisted crates and wheeled bags full of sample sets up and down the nicer urban streets. The fount of the empire's knowledge was now owned by the successful colony. Sears had its own competitors such as Collier's and Macmillan, and various Boy's Own and Everyman series clogged school shelves. "Jurisprudence" and "Iceland" opened themselves under the eyes of curious children, who however couldn't be told too much. These children, now grown, remember with sticky shame the way their fingers tacked across the pages of those antique contraptions.

In addition to general encyclopedias, which covered every topic imaginable, children read concise and specific encyclopedias such as those about buttons or barbed wire. While buttons may have gotten a brief mention in Grolier's *Encyclopedia Americana* under "Fastenings," "Costume," or "Closure," the *Encyclopedia of Buttons* outlined "Horn Buttons," "Animal-Shaped Buttons," "Lost Buttons," "Viennese Buttons," "Industrial Buttons," and "Buttons Used in Famous Crimes." The *Encyclopedia of Dogs* listed the "Chow Chow" and "Weimaraner," as well as species of worms that infect dogs of all kinds. Ancient, disappeared breeds lived on in vivid illustrations. Obedient or curious kids learned the name of every kind of mushroom or geological formation while remaining blind to certain events in their own neighborhoods. Later they might read in an encyclopedia of the decade about the race riots thirty miles from the snug suburb they'd grown up in. The experience of reading about it was nothing like the experience of smoke and truncheons, but the encyclopedia cultivated just this sense of safe remove.

The modern era of the encyclopedia is characterized by the reclamation of territory by subjects once considered mute. Encyclopedias that once barely mentioned indigenous people were countered by the *Encyclopedia of Indigenous People*, which listed all their attributes and lost arts. Deborah Mulligan's *Women's Encyclopedia*, begun in 1983, exhaustively listed feminine counterparts to subjects enthroned in *Colliers World Book*. "Menstruation," "Pregnancy," and "Dish Washing" had their own entries, and were not subsumed under "Anatomy, Female" or "Arts, Domestic." An overwhelming lassitude suffused its pages, as of a woman with three children and two jobs, no clean diapers, a broken-down Honda Civic, only four minutes left on her phone plan until next month, and that feeling behind her eyes like cardboard.

The Boston Women's Knowledge Resource Center began a revision of the *Women's Encyclopedia* in 1997, adding topics formerly excluded such as plastic surgery, firefighting, and K-pop. When this project transferred to an online site open to all, it grew to some eight million articles, some as short as three words. What became known as *Wykipedia* linked to *Wikipedia* in order to add dimension to male-authored and male-slanted entries. For example the prime minister of France googled himself and was led to a bio he'd never seen before, which listed all his wrongs and neglect toward his family. The entry had been penned and posted by the eldest daughter of his former mistress. Where his honors and awards should have been, he found the heading "Lies and Shortcomings."

The dark web spawned its own encyclopedia, the *Murkipedia*. Children should be warned not to use this. Instead of spreading knowledge, the *Murkipedia* draws it from its users and destroys it. The reader plows toward the *Murkipedia* slowly, with great care, first downloading an untrackable browser, then searching for strings of code, and finally wading through obscenity-laced ads by hitmen for the dispatch of wives and creditors.

A teenager has memorized all the lyrics on the first five albums of a mildly popular band from Ohio. He passes by drawings of machine guns and low-res photos of holes put through motel windows. He types the band name into *Murkipedia*, thinking at last he'll get the truth about their origin. Instead he finds himself lying on his bed facing the wall, picking at the scabs on his chin. The members of the band tune their guitars aimlessly, then go back to playing video games. They've forgotten they ever knew how to play their instruments, and they don't know why they ever bothered. If they remember to update their blog, they'll see text and photos converted to a series of filled squares against a gray background. Their fans look at the tickets in their hands and can't remember why they wanted to leave the house. Dread and loss pour up their fingertips and infect their nerve branches. The parking lot of the arena where the band might have played stays empty all night, moonlight scratching white lines through the puddles on the asphalt.

Further Reading

There's no need for the encyclopedia article to be true, only to have the weight and sadness of truth. My professor Nick Gravenstein once asked if there were any questions, and when I asked one, instead of answering it, he suggested that I consult the eleventh edition of *Britannica*, the only worthy edition. It was a way of making me look stupid for having asked, and to make him look smart for being so precise in his recommendation. Nevertheless I thought he was handsome and witty. Even after he plagiarized from me in a public presentation at the college, passing off as his own work whole paragraphs from my final essay for his seminar, I wasn't quite off him.

Fallujah

It's not uncommon to meet veterans, some of whom tell you everything, some nothing. They go to massage therapy school on their full-ride veterans' stipend, they smile at you from park benches, they use their vast mechanical skills to figure out why that light is signaling some internal disaster in your car. You may have been warned to let them have a seat facing the door, and not to press them too hard if you're their personal trainer or phlebotomist or even just their cashier in the Kwik Trip. It's good to know that men and women walk among us primed to react strongly to things others of us can't see, as we don't have their experiences.

I met a man called Quinn at a poetry reading where a friend was on the bill. Quinn told me about writing a short story for his class at the local community college, and later he lent me the manuscript. In the story, a man sits in a waiting room before a medical appointment and keeps seeing a little girl behind a glass door. She sort of shimmers, hidden where the glass is transparent, but her head is visible the whole time. She looks at him. The man is sure the little girl isn't real. No one else in the waiting room reacts to her. They're all looking down into months-old copies of *Golf Digest*. Then the story moves to a giant mud hole. People are dying all over this mud hole, dropped into it, climbing out of it. Tire tracks cross it, in its dusty parts. Pits of water bubble, then dry and crack. His story described the texture of the baked soil, the heat under his helmet, the view of the mud from a distance, from close up. Sounds of people shrieking. It went on for pages, these precise scraps of vision of this mud hole, this bog, this shallow grave. This place, the story explained, was called Fallujah. The soldier in the story had been stationed there, in Iraq, at one of the worst scenes of carnage in the Gulf War.

The poet had read this story aloud to his creative writing class at the community college when it was his turn for critique. His fellow students piled on him. Why had he made all that stuff up? His story was like a caricature of a war story. It was inflammatory. It was disgusting. The writer should write about his own experience, and not borrow suffering from websites to make his narrator's experience sound dire and important. The other students' stories had been about waiting for their stepmom to show up in a far corner of the Best Buy parking lot, and about a girl named Laura's rough night after a break-up, and a kid who had cancer, and that kid's brother's feelings after the funeral, and about basketball, and a carjacking, and an old man who hates the squirrels who raid his bird feeder. It wasn't fair to make them, his fellow students, squirm with his second-hand pain. "Your story," one of them said, "brings us very close to the experience of the newspaper reader, who winces in outrage, and then turns to the sports section. It's cheap and ephemeral, this shock value from horrific eyewitness accounts, which are probably exaggerated, misunderstood, and distorted in translation. If there's anything you learn in this writing class, it should be not to write like that."

But I was there, Quinn told the class. I was in Fallujah. All that is basically from my diary. I was a medic in the army for two years. Now I'm training to be a nurse.

The class felt very sorry then for their assumptions that his shocking narrative was made up. Maybe because he was such an ordinary-looking small person, not particularly fit, not clean-shaven, they hadn't thought for an instant that he'd been in Iraq. Quinn laughed about it, telling me later. But I could see why he might think poetry was safer than prose. A better bet. To keep things short, and not so explicit. His story, he said, had after all been a piece of junk. Everyone thought they should write about their war experiences. It was really better not to.

Future

Conjecture based in both science and the world of the spirit suggests that in the future, everything will change, yet remain the same. The encyclopedists of the past declined to include a chapter on the future, feeling the most they could say was that the word *future* derived from *about to be*. A hope. A wish. And not the clanging of a lid down on your head, a sudden blacking out. *The future* is more of a grammatical term than whether that woman who looked up as you passed her counter will smile at you next time, and one day kiss your neck. How will my children survive after I've gone? Mothers have spent whole months with no other thought. But no one can say.

One day a woman woke up to realize that the roar of trucks on the interstate obscured the music of birdsong even though she was miles from the highway. If not for all of the people and their machines, their duplexes, their Shake Shacks, their Cold Fur Storage, their quick oil change shops, their Museums of Anthropology, their fishing trawlers and gravel crushers, she could greet the day listening to sparrows and crickets. The woman wrote this thought down as a rhymed poem, then recorded it as a video. Within ten minutes of posting it she had converted people on three continents to agree with her that reducing the human population by half would make living bearable for the rest. Her armed acolytes began breaking up concrete and shooting half the occupants of cars they stopped at their impromptu roadblocks.

Though the adherents of the Half movement thought half was a modest demand, those not persuaded resisted strongly. It wasn't possible to live peaceably alongside those who would bludgeon your daughter and your husband, leaving a wife and baby son as the surviving half of a family. And if more assassins came months later to take half of the half that was left, the mother, the baby? The Halfers hadn't thought that out. Those who would level floors six through twelve of an apartment tower weren't appreciated even by those in the garden level through five, though it was better this way than trying to take out the bottom of the building and letting the upper floors fend for themselves. "They only want half, but it affects all of us," the resistors grumbled. Those who wanted to live amiably with everyone were forced to defend themselves. "I want half of you dead!" screamed a gunman in a crowded bakery. Anti-Halfer vigilantes immediately shot him in the chest, as well as anyone who had seemed to agree with him. Through the strength of this idea, half died, one way or another.

Varieties of word play strengthened the concept. A woman pleaded "Have mercy!" when the cops pulled her over. They were checking for Halfers, and shot her over the difference between her *F* and *V*. Those who lisped trembled. Immigrants enrolled in accent reduction classes, or resorted to pointing and gestures where formerly they had rattled away in the language they had learned diligently. An eighth-grade history teacher paused at the front of the classroom, afraid a slip of the tongue would give one of the fervent teens the wrong idea. It became dangerous to say, "You have to!" or "Do you have any … ?" In this way, even the most mundane conversations touched on the world-political plight.

"Better half dead than half-dead," went the slogan of barely ambulant men finishing their night shift at a medical supply factory. Yet what resonated most as a movement of the have-nots against the haves worked its way up to the rich at the top of the pyramid. Statistically there were far fewer wealthy and privileged Halfers, but they made up for it by being many times more virulent than the meek Halfer boys who blew the leaves off their lawns. Retired tech gurus let half their domestic staff go, hopefully to starve, while making the remainder work twice as hard. The chicken salad didn't taste the same after the Venezuelan chef left, yet the Halfers proclaimed their willingness to suffer to enforce their ideology.

Neighborhoods of suspected Halfers went ablaze in the night. It wasn't clear if they had destroyed themselves or been set upon, but the fires were blamed on the Halfers either way. In killing or being killed, the Halfers fulfilled their mission. It was so satisfyingly complete. Though they only cared about Half, the other half, the idea's shadow side, made it whole. The Halfers torpedoed container ships carrying shoes and computer chips to bloated coastal populations. "We can't buy *anything*," the non-Halfers complained in the aisles of Sam's Club. This was hyperbole, as half the stuff was still there. But if the shelves weren't full, they might as well have been empty. It wasn't worth living this way. Now armed against attack, those who didn't endorse the Halfers' campaign nevertheless often killed themselves in despair.

The woman who had started the movement renounced it when she was diagnosed with pancreatic cancer. Every day journalists called to ask her if she was sorry. She was. They had lost count of the math, and used conflicting formulas to calculate how many had perished and who was left. Splinter groups advocated killing half of the half who remained, ad infinitum. Other factions projected a long-term dwindling, which the movement had started and now couldn't halt.

A young man claimed that the joy of feeling fully alive in the face of constant danger made up for his fear. Crowded shopping districts had emptied. The price of tickets to pro basketball had dropped sharply. People who remembered more of the previous era were less sanguine. When will a rain of fire come to obliterate this conflict? a grandmother thought, looking through her trashy jewelry for one good thing to pass on to her granddaughter. A cataclysm that took them all would at least be unbiased. None of her bracelets had been worth much at the start, and now they were nicked and tarnished. One had a dozen tiny diamonds spaced out around the band. Where one stone had fallen out gleamed a dark indentation surrounded by claws.

Gloria

THIS IS ABOUT GLORIA from American writer John O'Hara's 1935 novel *BUtterfield 8*: how Gloria sees herself, her wants, her wish to escape from being a creature so-called Yale men chase after. She's made herself into this desirable thing, and her affair with businessman Weston Liggett is the first taste of her own desire slapping back at her. So, something about female desire, very raw, and how it's been written out.

Clearly, the wrong place to look for female desire is *BUtterfield 8*. Even though it's all about female desire, and the come-uppance of one Gloria Wandrous. She drinks and has sex all she wants. That's why she stands out. She's willful and gets her way. But there's very little in the novel that would show you what that feels like to this woman who has taken Weston Liggett's wife's mink coat the morning after he ripped her dress off her. She wakes up naked in his empty apartment and finds some money he's left her on the nightstand. With her dress ruined, she takes the coat to get herself home in. The coat becomes a point of contention between Gloria and Liggett. He wants it back so he doesn't have to tell his wife that her mink has been appropriated by the woman he screwed in their marital bed. He is fundamentally dishonest and a coward.

The novelist too might be afraid to confront what he's uncovered in this scene of the ripped dress. It resonates in the protagonists' minds later; that much he grants. It's the moment that binds them. But the actual tug on the material, the soft shriek of the silk, he does not describe. He doesn't go into the rush Gloria feels in her sudden defenselessness, how her urge to cower transforms into her tearing at Liggett's buttons. Maybe there was an interval when both of them went from standing to falling onto the bed, where Gloria's reflection passed through a tiny gold-framed mirror Liggett's wife had hung above a landscape her aunt painted. Gloria catches her own eye, obscured by disordered hair, burning like a comet. John O'Hara takes us discreetly to the aftermath, not the act itself. The fur coat becomes the narrative engine. The reader is left with Gloria's unwritten sensuality foisted onto a gleaming garment sewn from dead skins.

The fur appears in a taxi as Gloria escapes Liggett's sumptuous apartment building in the glare of daylight. A couple exiting Liggett's building remark on the woman in a mink as the cab races downtown. It's clear they wouldn't have noticed her if it weren't for the fur she's encased in. Gloria's friend Eddie is startled to encounter the coat in his closet when she comes to visit that morning. It fills the narrow space, blocking out his wool lumberjack jacket and his gabardine trench. The mink creates its own darkness, as if the closet were empty and unlit, because of its dense brown. What a mystery, how something overflowing with surface allure can appear at the same time as a gaping hole.

Gloria is employed as a model and something like an influencer, paid to wear dresses not her own and appear at certain night spots. She's a trendsetter. Some of the women in her orbit are put off by her swearing. She repeats to one female acquaintance that men she knows refer to themselves as "stewed to the balls" when they're drunk, and this woman swishes away, outraged. She's never heard the word "balls" from a woman's lips. It's just not right. The guys, though, won't leave Gloria alone. O'Hara gives her a benighted mother, a rich and distant benefactor, and a single confidant, this Eddie character, the one man in the Yale circle she hasn't slept with. He sees her as a sister, though it's not certain that she sees Eddie as a brother so much as a relationship she has yet to ruin with her wantonness.

Much dialog, from which we might discern Gloria's state of mind. The following statements are all hers:

"I'm Gloria Wandrous."

"It's spelt with an a, and it's pronounced Wan-drous, pale and wan."

"Mr. Liggett. No, I'm waiting for some people. It'll probably be all right if you join us."

She's a bright chatterer. John O'Hara offers her words without the weight of chairs being shifted, throats cleared, or hands rising to bring whiskies to the mouth. At least in these bar scenes, O'Hara's is a stripped down style, straight dialog with little grounding detail.

"You're the kind of man that would have a mistress and insult her in front of your wife because you thought that would mislead her."

She's right about that. She's somewhat the truth-teller for Liggett. Gloria's own truth about herself is that she's bad. It's just no fun to be this beautiful woman who parties all the time. Her emptiness is matched by Liggett's emptiness, which shows itself in his lies and hypocrisy, his cringing from his own well-bred, well-washed self.

"Where are we going?"

"What do you think?"

"Don't swear at me. I'm going."

"Oh yes I am, and don't you try to stop me, if you know what's good for you."

"I just want to get out," said Gloria.

said Gloria. said Gloria.

She was there before four, and took a small table by herself and watched the world come in. A bad thing about days like that was to come out of a speakeasy in the afternoon and find it was still daylight. When Gloria heard the address, she guessed it was no love nest she was going to, and when she saw the apartment she knew it wasn't.

It might be a blessing that John O'Hara doesn't presume to give Gloria much inner life, and sets himself to describe what she shows the world: her snappy words, her impulsive cab-catching, and her choice of seat in a public space. We may note that when Liggett tears Gloria's dress, he's in fact taking aim at her livelihood. Gloria is paid to wear the dress he destroys. His ripping it down the front is like Gloria coming into Liggett's father-in-law's chemical factory and bashing vats and vials. While Liggett tries to explain later that the money he left her on the nightstand was to pay for a new dress, not for the sex, Gloria doesn't see it that way. Her pleasure has been tightly tied to her humiliation and to economic loss. When she displays herself afterward in Liggett's wife's coat, she's setting her price way higher than Liggett was ready to pay.

Women of Gloria's social set would not have had the resources to buy their own furs. Obviously. Gloria is not interested in being kept, however. Maybe that's why she's so curious to the novelist. She rejects what seems to be the only path open to her. It's presumably because she has something of her own, that bright, sharp feeling of her hand on Liggett's bare chest. The novelist fails to describe the dim light in which Gloria ducked her head to look down the tunnel between their bodies at the dark mass where her pubis met Liggett's. Then she turned him over to get him beside her from behind, tugging at him until he figured it out. So comfortable that way, and no need to look at his furious face. He springs to his knees, hauling her around the middle to get at her doggie style. She instead faces forward and sucks his dick, just a little bit, then settles on her back for him to go down on her. She holds him hard by the ears. Not with his wife, but with his chorus girls and waitresses the rangy Liggett has had some practice giving head. Maybe. Maybe Gloria had a few moments lying still while he licks her, thinking of some other time in the woods with one of the Yale men, and then is startled to stop thinking at all. Her inner landscape rearranges, and she hears her own voice escaping. It's all totally unbidden and undirected at that point. Once she comes, she grabs him by the hips and rams him into her, where he's done in a few oblivious strokes.

Never got to the doggie style but it doesn't matter. She lies beneath him, chin on his shoulder, dreaming. O'Hara didn't write any of that. He didn't note the momentary escape from care and the economic uselessness of this unsanctioned sex. No one can make Gloria speak or work or take on any duties for these few minutes of lights passing through her unconscious brain. Was it fun? If they knew each other better, they might laugh together. They fall asleep. Gloria wakes up a few minutes later and goes into the bathroom to make sure her cervical cap is still in place. The novelist has given her an earlier abortion, but doesn't disclose what she does about contraception afterward. Possibly Liggett had a condom. Possibly neither of them mentioned or negotiated the costs of this act. The pouring out of their desire for each other's flesh exists for a few minutes free from any consequence.

The balm of release from being the straightjacketed businessman is what Liggett has felt in his many extramarital escapades. That Gloria could seek this escape as well, and relish her own sensuality—it's as if the luggage rack or the hatstand spoke. How curious that this woman is out for her own pleasure, unlike all the proper wives, daughters and sisters she's surrounded with. She rolled him over and hissed in his ear, confident and happy.

History

During the diffusion of zinc cadmium sulfide over Minneapolis in 1950, two men entered the alley behind Northwest Bank. They unlatched the case holding the fogger. The case had been made up to look like an encyclopedia salesman's, with a faux-crocodile pattern. But where the salesman would have had gleaming brass hardware to demonstrate his prosperity and the prosperity of the publisher of the *World Book Encyclopedia*, the army had chintzed out and put on some dull secondhand latches. The men knelt down and struggled to flip them open. First Fred tried, then Arnie. Arnie got out his knife and worked it under. When they finally popped the case open, they unfolded the legs of the blower and screwed them into the base of the machine. Three fan blades lay in the red velvet of the case. The large one needed to be slotted into the device, once it was opened up. The men didn't know what the other two fan blades were for. Different grades of substance?

Forty-four years later, a woman came out to this same alley to have a smoke. Smoking had been banned in the bank, and this local regulatory action had created new habits in smokers. The ashtray on the woman's desk had vanished. She and her smoker colleagues crept down the back stairs and stood out here, looking at the gaps in the asphalt. The old brick of the nineteenth-century street showed through the potholes. Another woman stood further down the alley, at the back door of the mortgage brokerage. The two women's cigarettes crackled in the wind, ash pluming toward the corner. The bank teller nodded to the other woman, who lifted her cigarette in reply. This meant, fuck it, we're still here. They can banish us to the alley, but we're still smoking. This small victory belongs to us.

At about this time, a historian began writing a book on the history of Minneapolis. He considered the city mainly from an architectural perspective. "Many well-meaning homeowners," the historian wrote, "hoping to protect their dwellings and save themselves the drudgery and expense of re-painting, fell victim to contracting companies that specialized in re-siding wooden houses with tarpaper, asbestos shingles, stucco, and aluminum siding. Most of the re-siding obliterated the original decorative detail, altered the appearance of doorways and windows, and generally degraded the appearance of the old houses." This describes a neighborhood known as the Wedge.

Brewers, authors and waitresses lived in the Wedge, as did two brothers who would grow up to form the band The Replacements. A famous school for educating kindergarten teachers also found a home in this neighborhood at the turn of the twentieth century. Alongside the school, which taught folk dancing and maternal hygiene to prospective teachers, was a demonstration kindergarten where the student teachers could practice. It seemed odd to pour so much energy into children under the age of five, but Miss Woods of the Miss Woods School believed that a solid preschool education could form good citizens and help families learn English. What the children did in their own homes, no one could dictate, but at kindergarten they would wash their hands, speak politely, and play like friends.

Horses

Horses are in many parts of the world used as everyday conveyance and muscle—to pull plows, haul goods, and to carry passengers at a trot across long swathes of open country. Cars and tractors have not replaced them. The living and the mechanical beast of burden live together, the ratio of one to the other fluctuating due to economic and historical circumstances too complex to map. In Iceland, workers on horseback preside over herds of sheep. In southern Mexico you'll see a man ride his horse through the town any day of the week, maybe directing the passage of ten or twenty donkeys. It's unremarkable to see this fellow dressed in black and silver atop his dazzling bay, though it's surely enjoyable to witness the peaceable union of a gentleman and his transport.

To name the breeds of horses is to descend into a maelstrom of regional conflict. Most of the distinctions made between the breeds describe the kind of horse or pony commonly found in a locale. The Sardinian, the Dartmoor, the Poitevin, the Kathiawari, the Sumbaya, the Florida Cracker—these are the horses of these places. Their heads are longer or shorter, their manes shaggier or more refined, their coats dappled or consistently brown, depending on the breed standard. Know, though, that the black ones born of the brown breeds may be sold for meat rather than be allowed into the collectivity known as the Morgan horse, for example. The Spanish Riding School in Vienna admits one bay into its field of snow-white Lippizans, that breed of horse trained to leap and rear with military precision. The other Lippizans born the wrong color are sent out to remote villages for use as draft animals.

Horses can be fed hay and oats, but can also keep themselves going on free grazing. Horses in the wild must fend for themselves when it comes to plants that make them ill. If a farmer or horse breeder is keeping an eye on their horses' diet, this person will scour the fields to remove noxious plants. Perhaps the horse breeder trains young children in the area to discern and pull up the sprouts of foxglove and laburnum. In this way, horses are teachers of botany.

A horse expert must master much more than which plants to eradicate. Those who deal in horses have on tap an immense vocabulary of body parts, from the mysterious frog to hocks and fetlock, cannon and brisket. Each item of a horse's equipment also has a name. The horseman or horsewoman has learned to identify the individual parts within the profusion of buckles and straps, combs and clippers. This person also knows the types, brands, and raw materials of the oils and whetting stones designed to keep the implements in good shape. Horse tack and harness is a specialized industry. Fortunes have been made solely on the manufacture of horse-collar pads. Middlemen buy the metalwork, the soft goods, the leather pieces, and sell on the whole set. You can't expect one little harness factory to spit out cast metal objects, felted wool, rubber, and leather. It's just too much.

Children love horses, seeing them as a route to power. Those too young to ride caper around on rocking horses, or gallop around the dining room on a stick with a horse's head on it. Children of American suburbs may graduate to riding a pony in a circle in a mall parking lot when a little fun fair sets up for the weekend. When hefted onto the sturdy beast by the attendant, the kid feels she is actually riding, and at last in control of her destiny. Her horse is in fact tied to a post, and walks only counterclockwise. If the kid goes back to riding the stick with horsehead, it's unclear whether she's playing at being the horse or being the rider. In a young child, this split consciousness causes no concern.

Elsewhere, kids ride actual full-size horses with their moms or older brothers, no big deal. Even at the age of three some children will have been set up in a special saddle and grasped the reins. They say riding is in their blood, but it's in their physique. These young riders develop the set of oblique muscles that stabilize the spine and connect upper body to lower. It seems like a natural advantage, this sense of balance and core stability. But it's an advantage only in a world where strength and agility outweigh the ability to send missiles via drone to blow up truck convoys and fuel depots from thousands of miles away.

Children of the mid-twentieth century sat astride plastic horses strung up on metal frames with springs. The child riders made an ungodly squeaking. This type of rocking horse in motion sounded very much like the noise the kids' parents made when they were upstairs in bed on Saturday mornings, the kids below watching TV. The metal springs protested, the headboard knocked the wall in even beats—one shrill but muffled cry, and then stillness.

Today you can visit the rocking horse of King Charles I of England, preserved behind glass, a stubby wooden thing. The kids who rode plastic broncos think themselves far superior to that miserable prince, who scraped the floor in a corner of his nursery on that stunted, unlifelike block of wood. In the 1970s, children were able to squeeze a quarter out of their mother for good behavior in the shoe store and ride a coin-operated horse that came to life to wheeze and buck. A whole year might pass between one particular child's rides on this thing. But almost every day, some kid rode it. Eventually the mall owners placed a metal race car with a bucket seat next to the horse machine. The car also juddered side to side and up and down, the same motion as the horse. When faced with the shiny competitor, the fantasy of the horse began to fall away—this repetitive mechanical action couldn't really be what riding a horse was like. The horse ushered in doubt.

Most of these mall shoe-shoppers had never been near a horse, though their grandparents might have farmed hard acres in North Dakota. These children saw horses in Westerns on TV, and so knew whinnying, bucking, galloping, the rhythmic thrum of the mounted battalion on the move. In Sumatra and Slovenia, horses pulled loads of logs, while in parts of the world that used mechanized equipment, horses continued to be bred and trained solely to imitate these past practices. Movie cowhorses had to be produced so that movie cowboys could sling their legs over them. Orson Welles had to deputize someone to provide the carriage horses in *The Magnificent Ambersons*. The same woman, so organized behind the scenes, who made sure of the authenticity of the Amberson ladies' replica bonnets might also have had to secure the coachman's black gelding. A whole subspecialty rose up in Hollywood, the procurers of horses to play horses on film. The Hollywood stables looked for especially calm and patient ones who could stand the firing of guns near them. Though on screen the horses reared and snorted, seeming to show their high spirits, in actuality they were almost pets in their amiability and willingness to please.

British period dramas of today require huge numbers of horses to replay the actions of horses of past eras. Carriage horses must be bred and trained in order to portray horses pulling expertly replicated broughams, gigs, char-a-bancs, hansom cabs, and so on. In a recent episode of the BBC's "Sanditon," a British army regiment arrives, a hundred men in red coats on horseback filling the small seaside town with eligible bachelors. These military heartthrobs are also a kind of relic. Later the heroine and some others ride in a coach to the home of a child who has been struck by a horse's hoof. Probably few doctors alive in the modern Western nations know what such an injury would look like. The writers and director have paged through musty textbooks to get it right. The child actor moans, the doctor actor brings out needle and thread, the beautiful star actress looks on with the calm grace her character is known for.

After the scene has wrapped, the actors snap out of it. They fling off the tight clothes, laugh, and say "fuck yeah!" One of the actors is American, and resumes her careless, ugly American speech patterns. The others try to imitate her. Though they have keen ears and excellent accent training, when they try to talk like her, they sound like mobsters.

Outside, in a metal shed set up as a temporary stable, the carriage horse actor goes on being a horse. The horse munches hay and snorts in recognition as her caretaker passes by. She lowers her head and rubs her ear against the side of the stall. The horse is unaware that her existence is just a role and not reality.

Insects

IT'S A REASONABLE PROPOSITION. The benefits of eating insects should be fairly obvious: a source of protein that thrives in dense, crowded living conditions such as a cage or box. Their bodies harbor minerals, vitamins, and other organic materials that have been depleted from our soils. They lack the staring eye, the humble head, the recognition of their own death, that other meat sources plague us with. Not that they don't have eyes, but insects don't tend to grasp our souls with them.

Mostly they eat us, not the other way around. They inject us with poison and suck our blood. They chew up our corpses and return us to the earth. They strip our flesh. They whiten our bones. They eat books in our libraries. Embedded in the binding, they come out at night and erase certain vital lines. We already eat them accidentally, the weevils ground up in the flour, the gnats stewed in the tomato paste. No model wedding cake in a bakery window is complete without its coterie of fly corpses at its feet. Allowable percentages of wing parts and mandibles are part of doing business in a rye cracker plant. You can't even see those little black legs and hooked feet. We should go at it whole hog. What's stopping us?

Cicadas sing for us. Roaches provide interest to the dark corners of our motel rooms, scurrying out of the way of our sudden light. Everyone has a soft spot for fireflies, bearers of suburban nostalgia. Ants clatter around our dropped crumbs when we eat our hasty sandwich in the concrete plaza outside an office building. They don't seem to fear our eating them. They would never suspect we're about to sweep them up with a broom and drop them in boiling water, then dry them on a grill.

Cricket flour. Cricket-flour patties. Cricket flour added to school lunch macaroni and cheese—kids thrive on it. Do they become soulless? No, more communal, singing in harmony. Free from care.

Maggots grown in cheese likewise flavor themselves, so that the cheese tastes like cheese, and the worms taste the same, except for their prickly packets, the texture on the tongue. Some sailors had been

> Of course, the question is why it is necessary at *this time*
> grasshoppers turn an appealing red when boiled or fried

but fighting, as always, that horror movie image of a mouth open on white, wriggling grubs, the legs moving, little spots of eyes staring out, so that the consumer in this case might be called the victim.

The worst industrial bug farms, mats of crawling bodies living their days out in filth, would be welcome to them, a step up. No calloused, self-hating men are needed to round beetles up for the slaughterhouse, running among them with stringy arms held wide, snarling: "you shitheads, you dumbasses." We can blind them or gas them, trim their horns or dock their tails, and they don't feel it, and don't mind. They eat their own young, crunching up eggs or little larvae, and this doesn't put much of a dent in their overall reproductive capacity. We can shut them in a giant three-story concrete bug factory with a dead elk and come back months later for the harvest. They aren't aware of our neglect. They want nothing to do with us. They don't seek to know us, or to harm us. Grasshoppers will never look at us with that mournful eye, head turned to the side, that says, "I've done everything you asked."

Invasion of the Body Snatchers

It doesn't make any sense, but let's stop asking for rational explanations. Let's just say that giant pods, like big rolls of tobacco leaf, start appearing in a small California town's basements and back parlors. When the pods ripen, human beings step out of them, identical in every outward aspect to the citizens of this community. But they're not the same as the bodies the pod bodies replaced. The difference is on the inside. These new vegetal beings have lost all their passion and curiosity, their anger and pettiness. They walk down the street with a smooth calm. "Breakfast's ready!" calls the pod mother, in a voice that imitates exactly the tones of the mother she's replaced, but minus the strumming of love that formerly animated it. She made breakfast because it's the appropriate and expected thing to do, not because she cares for her children, husband, and elderly father-in-law.

We might interrogate the filmmaker's sense that the original mother provided breakfast out of love for her children. In fact, it seems like the original mother is as much of an automaton as the one who replaces her. We've arrived at the "labor of love" in which a woman's affection for every boyfriend, neighbor, and relation in her orbit gets transcribed instantly into long afternoons of writing thank-you cards, evenings of chopping celery and nights of toweling up vomit. *Invasion of the Body Snatchers* doesn't stand much scrutiny. The main characters are a handsome doctor and the woman he loved but lost years earlier. Both are now disgraced by the dissolution of their marriages to other people. You'd think the whole town was hammering on them to bring them together again, as if their unattached status was a plague to be defended against. In fact this is the real crime, committed offstage before the action begins—they've separated from their spouses, and are now living as single adults, possibly sexually fulfilled through brief encounters. They have money to spend on clothes and restaurant meals. They're flashier and jollier than the drones around them, who clomp to their jobs in the hairbrush factory to put food on the table for the little ones. If anyone was going to say, "Fuck this chemical company!" or get upset about the burning of houses on the Black side of town on certain summer nights, it might be these two. Though even if you watch this movie straight through five times, you won't see a single dark-skinned character. Just a farmer who might be Italian.

I saw this movie when I was in my twenties, in a theater in Oakland. The woman, fleeing the pod people who want to end her autonomy, cries to the handsome doctor, "I want to have your children!" I shrieked with laughter. The pod people have already got her. She's already wearing the right length skirt and modish heels. She reads softly cultural magazines. She's pinned her self-worth on gaining an appropriate husband, and this one will clearly do. She's been created, as a character, with no surprises. The pod people don't stand in the way of anything she's been raised to want.

This shows you how generally inappropriate my reactions are to the backbone of my society. The character's thought for her future family seemed inexplicable to me at the time. Her delivery seemed to have come from much coaching, though it was an echo of a desire that's quite common. I just hadn't felt it yet. Some women have never experienced the desire to have some handsome man's darling children. Good for them. They're ahead of the game, though I'm not sure this sensibility, or lack of one, gives a woman a corner on freedom.

Jest

Even though I was the youngest of us three sisters, I moved myself out of the family home before Althea and Vicky did, and made it a point not to return. However, one summer I was between places while my parents were going to visit our aunt. Mom asked me to stay at the house and look after the dog. "Vicky's there anyway, she can do it!" I complained. I had my eye on one of my friends' spare couches as a putative address, while I was in fact hoping to stay with a man I had just met. Being in town for only three weeks was the perfect opportunity for a summer fling with a lithe, handsome dude who read tarot. As I could not say this to my mother, my mother could not say to me that Vicky was drunk or high most of the time and couldn't be trusted with our poodle, Duchess. She explained that after Vicky had quit the warehouse job a family friend had struggled so hard to place her in, she was pretty downcast. Lately Vicky stayed up all night and slept all day. Duchess needed to be minded by someone with a more regular schedule.

My mother had given me instructions about her flower bed, which I disregarded. At that point in my life, I was more on the side of the weeds than the dahlias. After dropping my parents at the airport, I took their car to another town to meet my old high school friend Shira, and from there, to find her friend Tonya and Tonya's friend Piet. A place I considered unsurpassingly dull with its identical houses behind chemical lawns, its broad highways that had to be dared to get even to the grocery store, condensed down to one humid living room where Piet and I sat on the floor discussing the freedom of our preagricultural ancestors. The glint of his teeth in the unlit room and the perfume of Shira's clove cigarettes floated us away from the grid of postwar bungalows. While we were discussing all that had led to this preposterous spectacle of civilization, we felt we had left its constraints behind. We delighted in the unpoliced zone where the skin of our arms met. At five the thunk of the newspaper hitting the front door woke me from a dream, still on the floor, leaning against Piet's shoulder. I drove back to my parents' house, exulting. I let Duchess out to pee and gave her breakfast. If the bathroom door clicked closed after I lay down in the spare room, that would have been my sister.

The four of us met a few days later at a park, and the next day Piet invited me to tour the grounds behind an abandoned paint factory. Both times I packed up at dinnertime. Duchess was waiting. "Can't your sister take care of the dog?" Piet asked, holding onto my wrist. I laughed and shook him off. He was to come by the house on Friday. Then we would have more time.

"Good," he said, and the whole fantasy of our affair created itself in the air between us, as if we'd already been to bed and gotten out of it, felt the rush of want and its draining, experienced the delicious staggering of parting while our passion was still beating us toward each other. I made sure he had the address and could differentiate between the similarly named Streets and Courts and Ways he would encounter.

Nevertheless he was late, confused by the near identical houses ringed around the cul-de-sac, but the wrong cul-de-sac, even though I'd warned him. We walked Duchess, ate moussaka I'd made myself, and at last departed for the room that had been Althea's before my mother converted it to a serenely characterless guest bedroom. We woke after midnight, the moon shining through the window because I hadn't drawn the blinds, to a crash from the kitchen. Vicky had knocked the moussaka to the floor and broken mom's casserole. "You shouldn't have left it out!" she said. "You shouldn't walk through the house in the dark, blind drunk!" I replied. We were both correct, but I was the one to clean up the mess, being much better at it.

"Whose car is that?" she asked.

I didn't reply, but went on ruining my mother's beautiful kitchen towels with the moussaka. These towels weren't actually meant to be used for cleaning, and she kept other, rattier towels elsewhere, but I couldn't be bothered to dig them out. I may have said something as original as "None of your business" to Vicky's question. Piet's sweat coated my skin, and his semen ran down the inside of my thigh as I dumped the crockery fragments into the trash. Vicky had not come out of her room while we were eating, though I think she was awake.

If only Piet hadn't had a roommate in the place he was subleasing, we could have spent all our time there. We went out with Shira and Tonya to hear music, and to see Tonya's teacher's play. I was amused by how decorous we were in their company, and how even accidentally brushing his hand rocked me with sensation. By his third visit to my parents' house, Piet knew to come straight to the bedroom, where I immediately took off his shirt. We might have made sounds to rival the snarling of the raccoons in the garbage cans, as if we were totally animals and wouldn't ever get up later and drink coffee out of white cups. Piet had to leave by five to get ready for his work as a messenger in a law firm. The legal system and its air-conditioned offices didn't exist when we pressed into each other. Neither did the return of my parents, and my impending departure for California.

Though I ate and washed dishes and did my laundry in the same house as her, I totally ignored Vicky. I spoke more to Duchess than to my sister, continually telling her she was a good dog, the best, the smartest, while turning my head so as not to have to see Vicky's uncombed hair. She could eat what I cooked if she wanted to, though she had her own routines with cereal and ramen. I gathered she'd adjusted her schedule especially to avoid dinnertime and its perils of eye contact and speech.

I should have wondered what she was doing up at five in the afternoon. First she ate a frozen waffle, then she flopped in the living room listening to Pink Floyd on headphones. I took Duchess out back to play fetch, noticing how my mother's hanging petunia basket had wilted under my regime. I felt proud of myself for deciding to give it some water, though I thought it was ridiculous that I was expected to balance on one of the patio chairs to get the watering can up there. I hadn't heard Piet's car, and was surprised to find him standing in the kitchen when Duchess and I came through the glass sliding door. As my eyes adjusted to the indoor light, I took in his stiff expression, holding something in as he knelt to pet the dog. Normally we didn't need to say hello, but greeted each other with the wordless murmurs that picked up as soon as we embraced.

"What's up?" I asked, as Vicky passed the kitchen and slammed her bedroom door.

"She looks so much like you," he said.

"No she doesn't! Are you kidding? When did you even meet her?"

"I thought she was you, in the headphones," he explained. She hadn't stirred when he came in the door. Her eyes were closed, her lips moving. He didn't say that he'd bent over her about to kiss her, just that he'd mistaken her for me, and startled her. He let that word "startled" stand for a series of movements that might have happened, maybe a hand pressed to shoulder or hip, mouth to lips, and then the drawing back as Vicky's eyes flipped open and she shouted or gasped. He apologized as he read my outrage. He had already told Vicky he was sorry. He would tell her again, he said. What could he say?

"It was in jest," he said, a strangely formal wording contradicting how he'd already explained himself. This made me think there was more to it, that he'd spent some time with the semiconscious woman in the headphones before realizing she wasn't me. Had he lain down next to her on the couch, or lifted the heavy cup of the headphone and whispered something into her ear? His cheeks looked pale under the harsh kitchen track lights, and all the suppleness and radiance I'd seen in him in our previous meetings had drained, leaving a shell of awkward, shifty-eyed boy.

Our mother had sometimes commented on how alike Vicky and I looked, though she said I had "more contrast." I thought she was only ever saying this to make Vicky feel better that she was as small as and then smaller than me, even though she was older. Mostly our mother went the other route and wondered to me and Althea what had made Vicky turn out so different. She blamed chemicals our father had worked with before we were born. She wondered about the milk that had been tainted with flame retardant, a Michigan scandal that had come to light only after us three girls would have spent months drinking the white poison. Then she blamed herself for having let Vicky drink coffee when she was little, because caffeine had stunted her growth. She never admitted that all three of us would have been affected by the chemicals on our father's shoes, by the milk contaminated with polybrominated biphenyl, and even by the coffee, which was after all only a tiny bit of coffee in a mug of milk, sweetened with sugar. We had all drunk it, just Vicky a little more than me and Althea, that's all.

 I meant to make Piet tell me exactly what had passed between them. What was this jest, how had he clowned around with Vicky, and how had she taken it? But I stayed stuck on how he'd said Vicky and I looked alike. I was certain that we did not. Though we might have had similar frames, and hair approximately the same color, I was lit up where Vicky was hunched in on herself. She was a drunk, miserable loafer, while I had enormous potential of some kind I hadn't deciphered yet. How could this man, or anyone, mistake us? It seemed so unfair for him to associate me with Vicky at all. Vicky and I had hardly had a conversation for the two and a half weeks I'd been dog-sitting. She was not at all like me, and I was not like her. Whatever resemblance Piet had seen was only because he wasn't really looking. Thank god I was leaving in a couple days, and I'd be able to put this foolish infatuation with Tonya's friend behind me.

Klaprothium

CADMIUM LAY IN THE EARTH FOR AGES before anyone thought to distinguish it from other ores and name it. A Prussian inspector general called Roloff visited a provincial outpost of the territory under his control, suspecting the local druggist of adulterating cosmetics with arsenic. Herr Roloff arrived in his own carriage, muddy and tired, and immediately arranged his notes and files on the table under the window. The low sun, pushed behind clouds, made barely enough light for him to read. He sent the maid, who looked about nine years old but was fourteen, to find a lamp. She came back lugging a large lantern. "Very good," he said, but he noticed that hay stuck all over its bottom, glued on with dried manure.

The next morning, Herr Roloff visited the factory that was producing the suspicious zinc cream. The owner walked him through the production rooms. The men at their benches kept their eyes down, though they said "Good morning" when spoken to. Vines had grown across the windows of the workshop, limiting the light. The inspector general recommended that the plants be removed, and the windows cleaned, inside and out. But the dim light was not the root of the problem.

Herr Roloff and the factory owner, Herr Hermann, sat down side by side at the testing table and went through the steps together. Herr Hermann might have been a country mouse, but he handled his materials with skill. His vials shone, no specks of dust spotting them. He showed Herr Roloff the rods and dials he had forged himself, adapting older tools so that he could adjust the blue gas flame more efficiently. His hands moved with stodgy competence, practical, not mysterious. Every fault Herr Roloff had prepared himself to witness came at him as its opposite, as improvements and ingenuity. Herr Hermann explained each step of the reduction, pitching his voice just between condescension and camaraderie, not quite sure of the inspector general's specific knowledge. The inspector general held a named chair at the university, but you could never be sure if these folks were not entirely occupied with the theoretical. At last Herr Hermann tilted his beaker toward Herr Roloff, revealing the yellow substance left behind when the reduction was complete. It was not arsenic, he said. The two agreed that they were in the presence of an unknown metal.

Herr Roloff and Herr Hermann kept up a correspondence, the provincial industrialist performing various tests, the esteemed scientist conducting duplicates of them back at the university. The factory owner was afraid for the reputation of his goods. He wanted to be free of the specter of contamination. Herr Roloff wondered what to name the new substance. He had visions of goddesses. He wanted to name it vestium, after the goddess Vesta, or perhaps cadmium.

Then a rival doctor, Klaproth, got involved. This Herr Klaproth replicated Herr Roloff's work and improved it. At first, Herr Klaproth's intervention seemed to give more credence to the discovery of the other two. The three of them bounced letters back and forth, studded with drawings, formulae, and asides asking after each other's children and ailments. But then Herr Klaproth suggested to the academy that the new element be named after himself. Even though he was clearly the third man on the scene of the element's discovery, this interloper wanted the new substance to be named Klaprothium.

Labor

In most cases before I start writing, I need to wake up the computer, and it makes a quiet protest. The machine takes a long time to cough up a thumbnail portrait of its mistress leaning against a pile of wood, and reluctantly offers a space below where I can type in my password. Then the screen goes black. Meanwhile its corpus teases me with a small crackling sound, as if deep within itself gears were rotating against other gears. I know those gears don't exist. Lately the laptop has been pausing, just nothing going on, for long enough that I can go into the kitchen and eat some crackers, come back, and it still hasn't budged. I might not be able to write at all today, I think, if this thing fails. At last a flag unfurls. It's a notice from the manufacturer of my antivirus software. Once I've read this notice, I can dismiss it, and the computer goes back to its labor on my behalf. The noise it makes next comes from our interaction—the actual physical tap of the keys.

A little girl lying on the heated floor vent of her aunt's house reading a horse book, I might one day write, sees herself riding away on a roan stallion. She outpaces the lack of groceries, weekly fights between her mom and her mom's boyfriend, and the teasing of two boys at school who call her "pig nose." Whether she imagines herself as the horse or the human, or a mixture of both that she doesn't bother to contemplate, this reader experiences a joyful rise: a situation that was unbearable becomes a victory. The horses in the books she reads motivate and cure. A horse lying in a river, laid low by sudden fever, gets up and gallops off—a fractured family is now a prosperous cattle-ranching business. A young groom bonds with a horse so dangerous he was about to be shot—the horse was only misunderstood, and now he's a derby winner. A wild horse is torn from his herd, but finds a new home where he salves the loneliness of a deserving child. Only *Black Beauty*, by English author Anna Sewell, goes the inverse route, exposing the powerlessness of the horse and its dependence on its owners.

In *Black Beauty*, the eponymous horse narrates his own story, one that poses maturity as an arc of misunderstanding and misuse. As the horse Black Beauty grows in power, he is confronted with increasing obstacles. He escapes a fire; he is galloped through the woods on a midnight errand to fetch a doctor. The horse is at first rewarded for his good efforts. But as he passes into new hands, his strength and good looks are gradually despoiled. Subject to the cruel whims of a fashionable lady, Black Beauty must pull a heavy carriage with his head forced up by a tight bearing rein. One night a drunken groom rides him hard over sharp stones, and Black Beauty falls.

Once his feet and knees are injured, the disfigured Black Beauty is sold to a London cabbie. Despite the good heart of his new master, the horse is forced to endure hours of standing in freezing streets at night, waiting for the cabbie's heedless clients. In London, Black Beauty sees his dear companion horse Ginger pass by, her head lolling off the back of the butcher's cart. Ginger has been literally worked to death. Black Beauty knows that this same fate awaits him. He is sold again, this time to a grain dealer, where he must pull a cart piled high with huge, heavy sacks.

Black Beauty was an immediate success on its publication in 1877. In fact, it was one of the most popular novels ever written, challenging the works of Dickens in total worldwide copies sold and keeping pace with *Bleak House* and *A Christmas Carol* in its many film and TV adaptations. Its author had scant time to enjoy the book's reception. Only a few months after her first and only novel appeared in print, Anna Sewell died.

Anna Sewell was raised a Quaker, though she and her mother lost faith in their sect and spent the rest of their lives searching for another. Sewell fell while running home from school one afternoon when she was fourteen. Though the diagnosis at the time was a badly sprained ankle, she suffered from a malady of her feet ever after. She was often unable to walk, her joints pained her, and she was stricken with weakness. Her bouts with illness, which may have been a variety of lupus, waxed and waned. Though lame, she retained the strength to ride a horse and to drive a carriage. After age fifty, she suffered a steep setback in her health and was confined to bed. This woman, almost too weak to sharpen her pencil, took seven years to write *Black Beauty*, her only book.

I brought my children to the video store at the time when video stores existed, and we rented a movie adaptation of *Black Beauty*. Our little family often had trouble agreeing on something to watch, and at times left the store empty-handed after a heated exchange in its aisles. I can't say which of the three of us was drawn to the cover, and which of us acquiesced. I would like to know, but none of us paid attention to this one of many episodes in our family saga, and I'm the only one who even remembers that it happened.

In the film, the horse reports his experiences, as in the novel, but this version is able to tell most of the story visually. The director has filled the screen with Beauty and his horse friends running across a green field. No words are needed to name this joy. The children and I sat on the couch in our bathrobes, me murmuring reassuringly as Beauty is led out of the burning stable. Though the kids had only been close to a horse one time when we took a hayride at a summer fair, they understood when Black Beauty got sick, and rejoiced when he got better. At last the story reached its crux. Black Beauty, pulling a cart loaded beyond endurance, collapses to the ground in exhaustion. As he lies on the cobbles, done in, his master doesn't try to help him. Instead the man jumps down from his seat, whips Beauty, and calls him lazy.

My younger child, a robust person who had already by this age witnessed countless confrontations between humans and aliens, good guys and robots, seen elves stabbed and elevators fall from their cables, who had once drawn me a particularly bloody representation of a prince in order to provoke me, broke out sobbing. It was a pure, unleashed grief like I'd never seen from him. He cried without the self-interest or anger that inflected his sobs when I didn't let him get his way. His eyes opened wide with a kind of astonishment that the tears were wracking him, like the way a cop in a movie looks down and finds his shirt soaked in blood, only then understanding he's been shot.

I had prevented both my children from watching movies I found upsetting, only to learn that I was the only one who was troubled by scenes of violence. The kids went with their dad to ride roller coasters and watch space monsters streak toward the earth, while I stayed away from these disturbing experiences. I was too scared even to go down a waterslide, while these two pelted toward the tallest one that would allow them. Neither kid seemed to flinch from explosions or undoings they easily understood to be engineered for effect. Now I had unwittingly led the little boy to a scene that truly moved him. "Black Beauty gets better!" I explained. "Don't worry, you'll see. He'll have a happy home again!" But my child kept sobbing. Now his sister and I consoled him and whispered encouragement. "You'll be okay. The horse is fine. Look, he's with his friends again!"

He kept crying. I held him to my chest, wondering what I'd done. This little boy, who loved running around and wrestling with his buddies, must have seen himself one day grown like me, with nothing to look forward to but unending strain. I had read *Black Beauty* years ago, though possibly in an abridged edition. I should have known this scene was coming. Somehow I'd blanked it out. I should have spared him. I should have covered his eyes. I may have had a vague notion that the story was sad, but I couldn't imagine that it would be so devastating.

Love

THE FIRE IN THE STARS BURNS IN US AS WELL. Never have I sprung out of bed so gladly as when I was in love with a man I worked with. Just to walk down the same hallway he had walked down a half hour before me restored my spirits. I watched his hands on the table top, on the occasions when a conference table came between us. Formerly we had been friends. Then I set him back sharply for what I thought was his inappropriate attention to me. I hadn't felt anything but vague affection for him up until that point. Once he stopped speaking to me, the feeling I'd had before transmuted, against my will and my own self-interest.

I fell subject to a constant tingling happiness when I was near him, counteracted by episodes of boredom and loss like being wrapped in concrete. All the good times with him were the past times, when I hadn't been in love with him, I realized. I used to think he was nice, and left it at that. Once he had stayed so long talking to me at the end of the work day that everyone else left, and the cleaner came slowly down the hall behind a whirring electric floor polisher. Only then did we get up from our chairs pressed alongside each other. We hadn't been kissing. Mostly I had been listening to him tell me things about his parents and brother and their battles with alcoholism. I was at that time married, and hadn't yet asked him to stop bothering me. After I fell in love with him, we spoke only when others were present, our voices pitched for the whole room, on sheerly technical topics.

Shulamith Firestone's *Dialectic of Sex* remains the most forceful reckoning with romance. More accessible, incisive, and outraging than Simone de Beauvoir's *The Second Sex*, Firestone makes clear that love between a man and a woman isn't possible without a great deal of exploitation. She published the book in 1970, when she was only twenty-five. It was particularly cutting toward women of that age, who felt themselves prey to great tides of feeling toward some man who coyly forgets his promises to call. One of Firestone's young readers fights back shame as she understands that the agony she endured when her beau kept her waiting for their Saturday dinner date is not an individual pain, private to her situation, but a dunking in a communal well. Her feelings, which made her curl onto her bed, her face against the wall, scarcely belong to her. Her anguished love for her boyfriend is more like the ratty bathing suit handed out by the attendant at her public middle school pool—well worn, unflattering, and roughly the right size. The system of patriarchy is arranged, Firestone writes, so that the man must keep the woman anxious about his love for her, and both parties suffer. How can he make a promise to a being that he's been raised to see as not quite human? The reader, who felt as if knives were being driven into her stomach when Jason flirted with her apartment-mate, isn't even a cohesive being to him. She's a collection of bodily attributes—hair, legs, tits and ass.

Far from blaming men, Firestone says, "It is dangerous to feel sorry for one's oppressor, but I am tempted to do it in this case." If women have been created as half-people, as things, then it's a predicament for those who must bare their weakness by enjoying their company. Poor Jason has to keep his feelings for Rachel in check, while Rachel drowns in hers. And the one who is aware of what's going on—it's Rachel who's bought the book, a battered paperback, with many passages vigorously underlined in ink.

With love comes labor, Firestone writes. This too widens Rachel's eyes. She's never questioned before why she has to pick up his dirty socks. Doesn't she have a degree in marketing? Didn't she take Accounting 1 and Accounting 2 before she switched her major? What force, unseen to her for her whole life, has bent her to be the one to wash the dishes, to do the laundry, and to buy a little basket for the remotes so they're not always losing them? She hadn't thought of herself before as volunteering her time and energy. When did I sign on to this? she wonders. And when will I be released?

Twenty-two years later, all she can see is unending rungs of labor, from the forced smile of the woman at the grocery checkout to the hum of the printer behind her boss's new executive assistant. Even when Rachel rests on the couch, thinking of nothing, she sees half a sweater she started knitting eighteen months ago, curled in a plastic shopping bag on the bottom rung of the coffee table. Who was she kidding when she thought she could knit? And what was she going to gain by giving the ugly, bulky thing to that asshole she was dating until last Christmas? Thank god that's over, she thinks. Next time, she'll find someone more suitable.

Michigan

The state of Michigan's motto is, "If you seek a beautiful peninsula, look around you." The phrase implies that you're searching for a beautiful peninsula and not for something else, such as an island, a river, or a lover who understands you. It puts the emphasis on the person evoked by the construction, rather than simply declaring the state beautiful. It brings up the settler mentality of those rapacious Europeans with their muskets, always scanning for a place to claim as their own. Michigan might have seemed to them not only lovely but safe, surrounded by the Great Lakes on three sides.

Imagine that a writer decided to license an artificial intelligence program that composes encyclopedia entries. This program has read all the encyclopedias in existence, or not read exactly, but moved its sensors over and analyzed the vocabulary and grammatical patterns of these pages. When fed a couple starter sentences, this program predicts the text that follows. It might produce *State Bird: Robin* and *State Flower: Trillium* as the more expected opening of the entry on Michigan. But recognizing that the encyclopedia it's been assigned to is a bit fanciful, it might layer in passages from *Nicholas Nickleby*, extruded of their meaning but reproduced in terms of syntax and sentence length—lofty Dickensian description of sunset and mood transposed into a passage about the battle for Fort Mackinac. This artificial intelligence program has never been to Michigan, never stepped outside its virtual cage and smelled wet grass. Only if wet grass has already been mentioned in an encyclopedia somewhere can the program come up with a description of the delicious, decaying scent of lawn care in an immaculate suburb of Detroit.

In the entry on "Michigan," either the writer or the artificial intelligence program goes on to say that thousands of lakes dot Michigan's surface. One of the largest inland lakes is called Indian Lake. Indian Lake is in Michigan's Upper Peninsula, much more beautiful than the lower, but seeming to be, if you look at it on a map, really just an extension of Wisconsin.

Native people have long been removed from Indian Lake. It's now in the hands of motor boaters, and perhaps a bible camp. A floating candy store ties up at the public dock on Thursdays and Fridays, and the kids go wild. Near Indian Lake lies Michigan's largest freshwater spring, Big Spring. The visitor to Michigan's Upper Peninsula starts to wonder about the generic nature of these place names.

A pamphlet published by a private advertiser in affiliation with Michigan State Parks relays the history of Big Spring, also called Kitch-iti-kipi. The name, declares the brochure, came from a legend about a Chippewa chieftain. A scheming maiden got him to leap from his canoe into the waters of the spring in order to prove his love for her. He drowned, and the spring was then named after him. Other legends follow: the lapping waves spoke to expectant Chippewa parents, gurgling names they should choose for their infant, like Little Fish and Big Eye; a drop of honey placed on birchbark dipped in the water would guarantee a lover's faithfulness; bark from the tamaracks surrounding the spring placed in a man's empty pocket would turn to gold at midnight. The brochure gives some alternate names for the spring, too, such as Sound of Thunder Water, though one of the most noticeable features of Big Spring is how quiet and still it is.

After laying out these stories in some detail, the pamphlet explains that these legends were made up in the 1920s by a man in nearby Manistique, who ran the five-and-dime there. The spring at that point was nothing but a black pond overhung with dreary trees. Lumber camps had used it as a dump. The store owner was the one who imagined how beautiful the spring could be, the trash removed, a narrow-gauge railroad bringing tourists directly from Green Bay to a landing deck for a glass-bottomed ferry. This businessman facilitated the State of Michigan's purchase of the spring as a state park. He promulgated the putative Chippewa legends only as a way to intrigue visitors. There's no way to know from the brochure if the various names he used in his propaganda were even Chippewa. Kitch-iti-kipi might have been conjured by the dime-store owner as something sounding convincingly Native, but that he made up on his own, in the lulls between waiting on customers and inventorying his merchandise.

A visitor to Big Spring, having glided over it in the glass-bottomed boat and seen the green limestone floor of the spring bearing its impressions of petrified trees, might wonder later whether the Manistique store owner had also made up the story of the two families, improbably named Palms and Book, who agreed to sell their land to the state to create Palms Book State Park. The lumberjacks who had fouled the pond's glassy water with their sawdust and ringed it with slashed logs and blackened cooking pots may have been his fiction as well. The Five and Dime proprietor too, who was said to have loved the spring so much that he would lock his store at any time to drive a pair of St. Ignace swells over to see the water, though it was seventeen miles away—he himself might have been created by the writer of the brochure.

And who created the legend of this legendary brochure? I can assure you that this brochure exists. I've got it right here on my desk. I've unfolded it, folded it up incorrectly, and tried again to get the cover page facing outward, instead of one-third of the map. It's a souvenir from a recent trip.

I grew up in Michigan, drove its highways, and ate at its Swedish-style smorgasbord restaurants. Only a few months ago I waited in line with at least a hundred others to be allowed onto the cable ferry that moves back and forth across Big Spring. The water was crystalline, viscous, unclouded all the way to the bottom. A woman had brought aboard her dog, a blue heeler. She held its leash tightly as it shoved its snout between the legs of some little boys. People held their phones up over the glass opening or over the edge of the craft. Despite their frantic jostling for a better angle, no one seemed satisfied that they'd gotten a good picture. It was impossible to capture the depth of the water and its strange clarity.

Motion

THE MOST REASSURING FORMS OF ANIMAL LOCOMOTION belong to the symmetrically four-legged. Dogs, horses, and sheep hit the ground with each hoof or paw in a prescribed rhythm, either in pairs front and back or the opposed corners. Their gaits can be classified as ambling, loping, cantering, and so on, a nomenclature related to the pattern of footfall and the height and force of impact, resulting in speed or slowness, hurry or relaxed moving around the earth. When this kind of four-legged animal comes to a stop, its feet stand planted like a desk or a dresser. Both the motion and cease of motion of these animals we most keep near us assure us of order and domesticity.

If the legs are of uneven length, then we have the hop or bound, as in a rabbit or a cricket, creatures that send themselves startling up and out, propulsion mainly from the back. Some animals have four legs evenly distributed, but the appendages are only weak and toylike. The lizard scurries along, too much belly interfering, as if its tiny limbs were wearing away. Animals dive into holes, in the ground or even under water, the muskrat poking its nose above the pond surface, tail cutting a line behind it, and then suddenly vanishing underneath. A squirrel bolts up a tree, an upward swarming, barely hanging on. This motion's major characteristic is the sound of the claws catching and releasing. The squirrel can repeat this motion downward as well, headfirst, usually with more caution.

The sideways scuttle of the crab, the sinuous belly rub of the legless. The flapping of wings, and the flapless glide. The hop and stiff-legged strut of a robin on the ground. A rooster does the same, picking up its feet as if they were curious implements, like the fork you're given at a banquet in a dream. A hawk might sit on the top of a telephone pole and not move for hours.

The movement of letters back and forth, tongues licking the stamps, fingers opening the envelopes, lips moving over the imprecations. Or the opposite movement, the lids coming down, the obstinate throttling of feeling, reaction, or comprehension.

The movement of an entire herd can be mapped in the aggregate. Each individual member pounds its delicate hooves, curling the knees, leaving the ground entirely in mid-stride. The photographer Muybridge demonstrated this airborne gallop, yet the motion of film has since become much more important than the motion of the animals themselves. The threading of film through the camera, the filing of the audience into the theater, the antics of creatures of all shapes shown on the screen. Men riding horses, clinging to them while they rear and buck. A slow shot of a woman's face, dawning with realization. The members of the herd spread themselves out with shifting distances between them, mothers slowing for their young, the faster ones making way for the more decisive ones when a change of direction is called for. The pattern of the flight of the herd represents a higher class of locomotion, a spreading, like a liquid, but in packets.

Water striders boat themselves across the surface of lagoons. Underneath, unseen creatures, millions to a teaspoon, wriggle along with the help of hairs, and gulping. The ciliates can divide asexually, a way of making more creatures. This too could be understood as a class of movement, the two stepping away from the one. The worm passes through the soil by eating it, combining forward motion with digestion. The motion of a fly in a living room combines with an audible element, the buzz getting louder as it veers toward our ears. The motion seems to have stopped. The poor thing might not have eaten for days. We find it belly-up on the windowsill, covered with dust. At some point, it expired of sheer weakness.

Fish leave no tracks in the water. Bats and swallows crisscross the evening air, so fast the animals seem more like marks scored with fine pens. Water birds can move through two elements in a single propulsion. Coots and diving ducks draw themselves under, rocking head down and then pulling the rest of the body behind them as if closing themselves into another dimension. The common mallard can't make that transition, and instead bobs its tail up while the head roots around unseen. This is a motion that makes everyone laugh, even babies in their strollers. It must be that halfway actions are humorous: they remind us of failure. Once while walking the cliffs over Lake Superior, I saw a cormorant glide through the air, skim the lake surface, and then dive under to continue its flight below the water. The water is so clear and shallow there that I could see the bird just as easily through the blue, continuing to beat its wings, but now this motion would be called not flying but swimming.

The centipede doesn't actually have one hundred legs, but imagine taking the time to count them, with tweezers, holding the thing upside down, every now and then breaking one off because you're so clumsy. Say there are sixty-eight. It swishes them in succession, having more in common with the twinkling of stars than with the agilely balanced placements of fleeting hooves. I almost can't credit the centipede with balance, far less the millipede, or the caterpillar who in its entire life moves through the leaf it was born on, utterly destroying its home while scarcely lifting its little pincers from it.

The lamprey is capable of its own exquisite shimmy, an undulation beneath the waves parallel to the current. Its body seems like a representation of water, as if it celebrated with its whole being the goddess who gave it life. Then it sticks its suckers on another animal, and the lamprey's locomotion becomes secondary to its host's. The host's progress becomes a fitful struggle, while the lamprey continues to make its soft flowing motions, the head immobile, spine flexible, like those little-girl Irish dancers.

My sister Vicky couldn't skip, failing at the switch-up symmetry but getting along with a galumphing left-leading gallop. It was okay while we were pretending to be horses, but in other situations, her clumsy gait embarrassed me. Also she couldn't whistle. Althea was a marvelous whistler. She pursed her lips and everyone near her dropped their shoulders and looked up as if to find the sound floating weightlessly from her, high and sweet like a piccolo. Vicky whistled stoically by hissing through her teeth, making a thick *shhh* sound I found repulsive. I couldn't whistle at all, and I still can't, mostly because I never try. There's a motion of the tongue against the teeth that I succeed at by not attempting it.

The cold-blooded animals move in surprising ways, but often don't. A lizard may sit stone-like for hours, and then whip out its tongue. The coral sits for its entire lifetime, growing only by getting larger and by shedding. If its intake and outtake are equal, it may on the average not move in any sense, though there may be some growth and some decline within the inert parameters of the median. Other animals may move every second of their existence, never resting, as is commonly believed of sharks. It could be true also of the tiny organisms pulsing through pond scum and seen only with a microscope. The biologist needs to sleep sometimes too, and can't stay up all night to determine if the creatures ever rest. Maybe they move only when observed.

Animals that hang from trees—the hand over hand swinging of the monkey, or slow shuffling of claws of the sloth—it's as if the trees have grown there just so these animals can have something to move past and through. The long grass waves itself closed over the panic of the rabbit, as if that were the motion, the shifting and settling and the long line across the prairie. The rabbit's movement itself is much jerkier, a moment by moment pounding of the ground. Animals that roll, like a barrel? Children play this way, rolling down a hill. Nothing in its right mind does this as a way of getting anywhere.

Names

ALMOST ANY WORD SOUNDS BETTER WITH -IUM affixed to it, becoming sonorous and serious, the way anyone, even a tubby man with a big beard, becomes more handsome on ice skates. The added height draws out the line of his torso, and that bulbous dude who can hardly move without flailing has been given the possibility of grace. So vestium—named for the goddess of the hearth, Vesta, not a sleeveless plaid wool garment—slides pleasingly. Vanadium too sounds like something to be swallowed. Plutonium. Compendium. Magnesium. These words have dignity, and look down on the rest of us. But we can only go so far with -ium, and Klaprothium can't be countenanced. The podgy Herr Klaproth got his mitts on a new element, now, thank god, known to us as cadmium. Klaproth duplicated and then improved the work of the initial discovers Herr Roloff and Herr Hermann. These two had suggested goddess-inspired names for their discovery, but Herr Klaproth wanted to memorialize himself in the yellow powder.

Invention is not finding, after all, but finding a use for. A daydream spreads across the mind, a collection of places, myths, information, and theories. It takes a man of action to make fruit of his inspiration. Herr Klaproth put himself forward, and shoved the others back.

The name *yellowcake* sounds delicious, and not harmful. Like you might find it on the ground, in this fabulous place Niger, where it's possible to manufacture atom bombs just by compressing the stuff enough, and so rule the world. The pronouncer of *yellowcake* can imagine themselves striding through Niger, perhaps standing out a bit because of the color of their skin, if they are a pale person, but nevertheless, this person who says *yellowcake* knows where to go and who to talk to. Pick up a bit of yellowcake. Like a petit four. It is in fact a term for uranium oxide. You could also call it partially milled uranium ore.

The documents that surfaced in 2002 about Iraq trying to buy "significant quantities" of a type of uranium mined in Niger, called yellowcake, were known at the time to be obvious forgeries. Nevertheless, the yellowcake story was fundamental to the rationale for the U.S. invasion of Iraq that followed. A senior official related that the shoddy nature of the fake disturbed him, saying, "It depresses me, given the low quality of the documents, that it was not stopped. At the level it reached, I would have expected more checking."

Please recall the anonymous parks official who objected to the diffusion of cadmium over Minneapolis in 1950. He objected to the program, or possible program, though none of his words are recorded. My source says only that this problem was solved when the role of parks commissioner changed hands during a new city administration. This parks official too might have been depressed after his demands for more information about the diffusion operation went unanswered. "Depressed" seems such an individual reaction, like a person who can do nothing but sit on the couch with the cat watching endless *Law & Order* reruns.

A person can become depressed when their romantic hopes are dashed, or after the death of a loved one, or for no apparent reason. Ann Cvetkovich, a scholar of the so-called Public Feelings movement, insists that depression can also be a political response, related to the collapse of an ideal or movement, the defeat of legislation one has fought for, or to a feeling that nothing one does makes any difference. "In a public event at the University of Texas shortly after the U.S. invaded Iraq," she writes, "the dominant response was one of incredulity, a seemingly low-grade or normalized version of the epistemic shock that is said to accompany trauma."

Numinous

When the U.S. Army diffused zinc cadmium sulfide over Minneapolis in 1950, crews of inspectors traced its path with sensors. They determined that it settled more rapidly in night deployments. The air was cooler and more humid after dark. The wind had died down. Fewer little boys kicked the points of their shoes into drifts of leaves across the sidewalk. In the evening, men heading for pool halls and workmen's clubs walked in straighter lines than the women who occupied the streets at ten a.m., pushing strollers, pulling grocery trolleys, or rushing off to find out what was up with their overly dramatic sister. "He's drinking again," the sister said. No surprise there, except for the *again*. When had he ever stopped? But it was much worse now, the sister insisted. She found lipstick on his shirt. They'd been so happy for three straight months, and now he was seeing another girl! These emergencies cropped up daily in Minneapolis, women climbing into buses or pattering down alleys, coffeepots percolating, mending left totally unattended in baskets or on tabletops as two or sometimes three women listened to these tales: She didn't know what he did with his paycheck. He came home and didn't say a word. She'd oversalted the potatoes and he slapped her and stormed out.

Then the women were late making lunch or doing the shopping. They ran out into the sunshine, scarves flapping, to pay the gas bill at the bank. It was due today. They had to buy pencils and lightbulbs and shoelaces. In 1950 that was three different stores. The nighttime streets were not intersected by these harried creatures rushing from place to place. After sunset, the men moved with efficiency toward the Chateau Lounge. The door banged behind them. Red and yellow lights shone out of signs for Gluek beer. "How's Cora?" a guy's buddy asked him. "She's good." After that, not much besides the lifting and sipping, or lining up of shots.

The cadmium lofted out of the blowers and vaulted onto the open balconies of the apartments on Third. It's not known who designed these buildings for such a climate, to have little overhangs with wooden decks and iron railings. The balconies were usable only a few months of the year. Rust radiated from the bolts holding the railings to the exterior wall. Their planks weathered and splintered, and were too weak for more than two or three people on them to feel safe. Girlfriends dancing out there in July got carried away with joy, and then screamed when they felt the wood tremble.

On the second of the night deployments, two men in coveralls driving a van with a huge brown rat painted on the side rolled up to an apartment house on Third and Crest. Though it was almost nine o'clock at night, they knocked with authority at the third-floor flat. The landlord had sent them, the more commanding of the two men told the woman in a bathrobe at the door. "I just got the kids to bed!" she protested, but they marched right into the living room and set up the sensor. She told them there were no rats here. She would have seen them. There were mice. And roaches. If the landlord wanted to do something about that, she would be more than happy. She went on chewing them out while one kid cried from the bedroom down the hall, and then the other. The third kid hadn't been born yet, but looked to be on its way in the next few weeks. The men studied the sensor readings, while out of the corners of their eyes taking in the mounds of laundry on the ironing board and the pots and pans all over the kitchen counter.

In the apartment below, a communist cell held their weekly reading group. They discussed the passage, "The bourgeoisie has torn away from the family its sentimental veil, and has reduced the family relation to a mere money relation." The leader of the cell gave an example of his uncle, who had set up a small company to manufacture electric motors. He wanted his sons to inherit it, but one of them clearly wasn't suited for the work. The uncle relentlessly criticized his younger boy, and became more of a boss than a father.

The other three in the cell nodded. They may have seen similar instances in their own families, but they had learned that it was not proper in the cell to relate to the readings too personally. It might be considered sentimental to talk about how unsentimental your own dad was. This dad didn't own an electric motor factory. He worked at a cardboard-box plant. The box factory worker's son had gone to high school and read Marx in secret, long before being recruited for the cell. He had not been with the troops that liberated Auschwitz, but had seen pictures. He couldn't be surprised by any crime, he said. The men in the cell focused on the future, when they would bring down the bourgeois structures that kept men in ignorance of their own servitude. But despite this forward focus, they acted as if they didn't expect anything. As their leader talked, they looked at their worn boots.

Because it was an error to make a personal, individual connection to the veil ripped from family life, education in the cell proceeded fitfully. The man who said the least spoke up only when prodded, to mumble, "I agree." The facility of their leader overwhelmed him. Their leader had been brought up to have opinions and to talk about them, while he had been walloped if he jabbered too much. He found in almost all cases that a squinting, aggressive look was the best way to communicate. The leader's paragraphs rolled over him. The leader of the cell talked about blindness, men who fumbled through their day with their eyes turned inward, as if they had voluntarily given up sight in order to endure the unendurable. "It's our duty," he told the group, "to be aware."

The men nodded. When the knock came at the door, they leapt to their feet and shoved their reading material under the twin bed that served as a couch. One ran into the kitchen and put the coffeepot on, while two others silently rearranged the chairs and dealt out a deck of cards to look like they were in the middle of a game. Their leader vanished onto the balcony, while the man who spoke the least answered the door. Here was their worst nightmare, army men dressed as exterminators, asking if the windows had been opened at any time that day, and setting up clearly bogus equipment. The taller so-called exterminator looked around with military authority, while the other man evened the legs of a tripod, casually shoving their card table to the side to make room for its gangly extensors.

This man peered at the dials and mumbled something to his apparent superior. The two communists in the living room acted as if they were lounging, unconcerned, while sweat ran down their faces. The quiet man clenched his fists to stop his hands from trembling. He tried to relax his arms from the shoulders down, muscle group by muscle group. If given a signal, he would leap to kill with his bare hands.

The taller fake exterminator declared that they needed to set the instrument up on the balcony. He didn't even bother to explain how rats could be detected with this contraption that looked like a barometer on legs. Or why vermin might be found on the deck.

"You can't go out there," the quiet man said.

His comrade gaped at him. He was no help.

"We're licensed by the city to do this survey. We need to get out on that deck there."

"No," the man said. He did his angry squint.

The two uniformed men consulted each other with their eyes. The quiet man stood. The other communist also got to his feet. The third communist came out of the kitchen with the coffeepot. Now they had a weapon. The quiet man sketched out the whole skirmish in advance, a blow to the chin of the taller man, his comrade getting the other one in the gut, the gout of boiling liquid stinging the backs of their necks, the card table knocked over as the three of them fired their legs back to kick the disguised army officers on the floor. These actions, as well as their long-term consequences, lined up while all five men paused. The quiet man kept his eyes away from the French doors to the balcony, where he would see only the reflection of his own grim mug, not the cell leader, possibly with an alternative plan.

"That balcony's really shaky," the man with the coffeepot said. "The landlord condemned it. Can't use it. It's not safe. We've got to get back to our game, if you're done here."

The two fake exterminators shifted their weight. They had been offered a way out. They weren't in fact clear what their remit was. They had traced the cadmium inside an elementary school that afternoon, from the roof to the second and first floor classrooms, and not a single teacher had challenged them. They'd been told not to attract attention and not to answer any questions. The taller man didn't like to take these guys' shit, but it might be easier to move on. He made a little click with his lips, and his subordinate began packing up the sensor.

"What game are you playing?" the guy carrying the sensor case asked, just as they were on their way across the threshold. The quiet man looked at the display of cards, four hands sloppily dealt, some with five cards, some with more, and a mess of cards face up next to the rest of the pack in the middle. Was it supposed to be rummy? Or crazy eights? Canasta? Bid whist? Given that their leader was keeping out of sight, they should have dealt only three hands. The jack of spades eyed the quiet man, looking like it knew what was coming. Next to the jack lay the seven of diamonds, a card standing for mockery and anger.

The quiet communist saw multiple sliding possibilities in the cards, how they could be shuffled and relaid to mean one thing, and then something completely different. Here were chances made into patterns, victories turning into defeats and then back again. Kings and queens were exalted in one game, and realized as a burden for their points in another. The twos and threes bore their lowliness in most cases, though in other circumstances the two promised love, the three, family. A numinous future fumed off the crooked card table with its hasty display. Anything could happen, depending on which card fell against which card, and who made the rules.

Already the price of this thought meant that the communist had delayed too long in answering the army man at the door. He swept his eyes down, away from the other's curious gaze, aware that everything he did and said was bringing suspicion onto the cell. Now the three of them were marked men, and their leader would cut them off. When just a moment ago the communist felt he had been building a world without the strictures of extractive labor, now his future was one of useless toil. He might go to jail, or just sink back into purposeless individuality, cut off from the movement.

He heard his own voice come out so low it was barely understandable. He muttered the name of the child's game to the fake army men: "Go fish."

The man lugging the equipment shrugged. His superior turned around and swept a furious glance at the room as he left. He must have noted the lack of beer or whiskey bottles on the side tables. There was no nudie calendar, no magazine photo of a car, pinned over the bed-couch. Even though the communist cell leader's book shelf held only three novels and a two-volume condensed encyclopedia, the shelf's presence at all hinted at someone who read and thought about things. Any other details of personality or comfort were not evident. The apartment failed to convey the impression of a hangout for regular guys on the block. In its spartan but messy masculinity, the living room of the second-floor apartment in the building on Third and Crest looked to the officer exactly like a place a communist cell would meet in.

Occult

SOME OF A CERTAIN DETERMINED BUT UNKNOWN POET'S favorite words included *obscure*, *occlude*, and *occult*. The openness of the *o*, even in a reader who didn't mouth the words but heard them silently in her brain, formed a vulnerability that leached into all the surrounding words. Like a type of environmental poison. So he thought. She, his mistress and muse, had written him a letter. She simultaneously pleaded with him and scorned him. It was exactly the kind of tussle that most attracted him, while it was happening and later on, when he went over it blow by blow. "I don't know what to do," she wrote him. "You haven't returned my call." She described the smoothness of his chest the last time they'd been together, and how the groaning of the bed as he got up and left the room had seemed like a voice speaking from beyond the grave. Not someone dead, but someone trapped in the underworld. The rusty complaint of the bedsprings woke her, she wrote, and she was confused to find him gone just when his voice was asking her to save him.

The poet sat down amid a lapping lake of papers and open books. The mess of others' words and his own scribbled scraps and printed-out works in progress comforted him. Everywhere, sentences and half sentences. Whole confident paragraphs and wispy notes—a few words, a dash, white space. Question marks.

To obscure is to drag dirt over, to make something difficult to see. *To occlude* is more serious still—to cover over, to eclipse. Now the one thing is in front of the other, and only if you had been there at the occasion of the dragging of the lid across its face would you know about the other, deeper entity. *Occult* is part of this series, and yet though it means hidden or secret, *occult* is the darkness that allows you to really see.

> She doesn't come at noon, *the poet wrote*,
> The day's too bright
> And not when I rest, or pause, or stare
> But when night locks up the streets, and the Wonder Bar doors slam closed:
> By the prick of departing brake lights, by the oil shine in a puddle,
> By scarce stars above the water tower,
> Then she comes to me.

It's maddening, the poet thought, that there might be an entire other world clothed in darkness that if we could only reverse, would reveal all that we need to know. He picked up one of the books that lay splat on its open pages: The filmmaker and occultist Alejandro Jodorowski wrote of the tarot that it was like "a domestic servant eternally working for a doctrine that was external to it." Everything was in the cards, he claimed. Right before his eyes, even grasped in his fingers. And yet it wasn't plain, but a lifelong struggle to read what was written there.

The poet moved Jodorowski's book aside, leaving it again face down. He shuffled some loose sheets of graph paper. He had torn them out of his daughter's geometry notebook. One sheet held a formula in pencil, crossed out. He pinpointed where his daughter would be right at this moment. He imagined her at her school desk, her hoodie flopped over her forehead, elbows shielding her on both sides, forming a triangle. Then there was another triangle drawn between him, his daughter, and her mother. That formation would remain, no matter what other lines were laid over it. This triangle ate into him lately, like wires across his throat. Or maybe it was she, his muse, his girlfriend, who these lines lightly sawed. She had asked to be released, but wouldn't go.

The poet closed his eyes. He had about half an hour before he had to take up the engineering technical-writing work that paid his rent. This mass of logical paragraphs waited for him to make it even more logical, better ordered, and free of error. Its demerits could be inaccuracy—the wrong illustration referred to, or a clumsy explanation of a force or process—or wrong punctuation, random capitalization. The engineers loved to assign capital letters to concepts they held dear. A whole afternoon had brightened for the poet when he spied the word Manifold bearing its resplendent uppercase *M*, as if the original writer knew that a fitting of several pipes inside an internal combustion engine also meant a whole that unites many diverse elements.

Poets

My friend Quinn's short story, when I later got my hands on it, was excellent. He was the poet who wrote a story about Fallujah, but his fellow creative writing students thought he was making it up. I don't know how they missed it. It was a great piece of writing. I told him so, and he thanked me.

You have to prepare your reader, I suppose, for what's about to hit them. They need to know right off that you're not putting one over on them. The poet Adrienne Rich was accused of stuffing her comfortable bourgeois life sketches with images of burning monks and screaming children, experiences which were all over the television, and which inspired thousands to clog the streets of college campuses, to bomb administration buildings and forego exams, but which she hadn't experienced herself. That is, she hadn't been in those napalmed villages, or burned herself up. She had no right to borrow this *foreign pain*, a critic advised her. She was nothing but an *armchair Marxist*, she was told.

Adrienne Rich left her husband and took up with a woman. Her husband then shot himself. Before his death, he had reportedly told their friends that she had gone crazy. Rich claimed there was suffering in being a woman, and in speaking about it. She was not surprised at the venom of her critics.

A poet's reputation after her death can take quite surprising turns. The poet Sylvia Plath has been revered since her suicide in 1963 for the boldness of her vision, and the way her mature voice incarnated out of an earlier husk of a more commercial, good-girl mentality. She had been someone who strove for the best grades and the rewards of winning contests. Her husband Ted Hughes, also a poet, suggested some of her early work was a little held back. Whether to please him or because a viscous lake of feeling was inevitably there for her to use as ink, her next round of poems had an alarming vitality.

It's hard to know whether other good girls in middle school would have been reading Plath's poetry if it weren't for her tragic life story. Her girl-with-a-breakdown novel *The Bell Jar* told the beginning of it. Her gassing herself after first making sure her children were safe in a sealed-off other room continued it. It seemed a fitting arc for a poet's life: struggle, success, marriage, extinction. Sometimes Ted Hughes's poet friends visited the couple and walked the moors with them. The poet friends didn't have a clue that the beleaguered mother was also a poet. These friends may not have said a word to her except "Thank you" when she took their coats, and "What little darlings" when she was asked to flaunt the kids at them.

Nevertheless, the idea that fifty years after her death, college students assigned to create a blog for their Marketing and Communications class would take a quote allegedly from Plath as an inspirational banner is hard to fathom. "The worst enemy to creativity is self-doubt," the poet is said to have said. By the time such a sentiment has made its way to the blog of the Marketing and

Communications students, no amount of argument, research, advice, or admonition will give her words the context that would provide a sense of irony.

A poet you might see on TV is Arabella Essiedu, the main character in the BBC miniseries *I May Destroy You*. This young woman has collected a bunch of her tweets into a book she self-publishes, called *Chronicles of a Fed-Up Millennial*. Actually, it's unclear whether her writing throws her into the poet category or not. Because they're tweets, they've got to be short. So probably poems.

Essiedu goes on a journey of self-discovery. She tries to figure out who drugged and raped her while she was on a wild night out that was supposed to be spent finishing the draft of her second book. The writer's muse is violent and faceless. Essiedu behaves pretty badly while on this hunt for her rapist. And she has a lot of trouble getting her book together. She fights chaos, and her own overwhelming need for affirmation. The poet must not only face her own vulnerability and humiliation—find her attacker—but keep on track amid many distractions. Essiedu is not a real poet, but a character in a show. An actual poet's struggles are not as cinematic, but are in many ways very similar, both on the surface and metaphorically.

Ted Hughes's version of Ovid's *Metamorphosis* remains one of my favorite books of poetry. Even though Hughes was not fluent in any language but English, he was well known for his translations during the long career he managed by staying alive and continuing to write after Sylvia Plath so flagrantly died. His loose adaptations in *Tales from Ovid* tumble with wrists, hair, bark, fire; human thighs dwindling into wolf's shanks; fits of lust like epilepsy. In these retellings of Greek myths by a Latin poet, now retold by an

Englishman, passion wreaks violent transformation. In Hughes's version of Ovid's story of the flood, the gods have decided to eradicate humans, whose sinfulness appalls them. Poseidon's sea nymphs explore a house formerly on dry land, now at the bottom of an ocean, where they

> ... roam astounded
> Through submerged gardens,
> Swim in silent wonder into kitchens,
> Touch the eyes of marble busts that gaze
> Down long halls, under the wavering light.

It's this word "kitchens" that gets me. It's so strangely, touchingly domestic.

Quiet

You might enjoy quiet in many places: the back seat of a car, the edge of a garden, a post office, a Dunkin Donuts. Elsewhere, an empty hallway, a library, a stairway landing. Sometimes it's quiet on a dead-end street, or in the alley behind the bridal shop. No noise intrudes on an ink and toner storage closet, or among shelves holding autumn-scented candles. A back lawn in the suburbs is often quite still, as are those little side passages that run between self-storage units. The bottom of the sea is quiet. So is the moon. The room where children complete their state-mandated test is quiet. The School for the Deaf is full of shuffling feet, but the lobby of a movie theater on a Tuesday night is quiet.

A railcar parked on the South Side of Chicago is quiet. Its chemical fumes and persistent leak have stifled any commotion on the ground beneath it too. A telephone booth in 2006 is quiet, and a mortuary, most times. An insurance agent's office is quiet, also an igloo, and a wood carving competition. The nursery where baby Ida sleeps is quiet. Honey Creek is quiet. The surgical recovery room is quiet. A commercial greenhouse is quiet, except for the hiss of the irrigation pipes. Sheds holding garden tools are quiet. On Wednesday evenings, the little town your new coworker comes from is quiet, and Thursdays too. It's quiet under a tarp, or in a cave, or in a ditch in the back of beyond. Barely any noise squeaks out of the east wing of the psych ward, because that's where the good patients are. It can be pretty quiet in the west wing too, after the bad ones have swallowed their drugs and all the doors are locked. It's quiet in the sperm bank, and in the evidence review room down at the station. The judge's chambers can be silent, and the elevator down to the street level of the courthouse, especially when it's full of people who are afraid of each other. Chernobyl ought to be making no noise by now. A temple overgrown with vines is quiet. It's quiet in the parking lot behind the Lutheran church. The airport is never quiet, but it sometimes seems like it is because everyone's ears are stuffed up, and the gigantic roar of jet engines manages to go unnoticed. A derelict truck is quiet. The page under a pen is quiet. It's the pen that makes the noise. A coffin is quiet, a grave is quiet, a jewelry store is hushed by plush carpeting. Inside the jewelry store's glass cases, not a sound.

A room where CDs are packaged is quiet, unlike the slaughterhouse. Thunder fills the space under the highway overpass, but you wouldn't know it to see that old guy sleeping there. You'd think it's quiet. The bookstore is quiet, the biblical figurines store is quiet, the further aisles of Home Depot, where lengths of beaded chain sit wound on huge spools, are deathly. The box where a poet stowed her old journals is absolutely uninterrupted. The time of the dinosaurs, or after the alien invasion, might have big pockets of silence, though the sound of ferns growing or buildings collapsing might mar these situations.

Rye Crackers

When the United States Army sprayed zinc cadmium sulfide over Minneapolis in 1950, men in coveralls tended the ovens in the famous regional rye cracker factory. Women in white smocks, their hair in nets, operated the punchers that gave the crackers their distinctive holes and perforations, while others watched the gray bread float by on the conveyor, plucking out misshapen ones for Quality Control to deal with. The loading dock groaned as workers emptied a railcar full of rye into the storeroom. A woman in a windowless office on the deck over the shop floor wrote letters to consumers who had written to her, saluting her as Dear Rye Cracker Co. or Dear Sir. Certain complaints she bundled and sent to the company's lawyers, Hellmuth & Johnson. Others she answered herself, enclosing coupons for more of the nutritious, slimming cracker. A mother had written in to thank the Rye Cracker Company for how nice her daughter looked in her prom photos with the weight she'd lost due to swapping the company's product for bread. Another wrote to say the taste had been slightly off in her last package. Had the recipe changed to include more salt? "I'd like to know, because my husband has been put on a low-salt diet," she wrote, in lovely blue ballpoint. Miss Vickers typed her answer.

She had memorized the paragraph about the company's studious control of sanitation and proportion at every step of the manufacturing process. She did not write about the variation in the human palate, that as a person aged, they began to taste less acutely. More subtle flavors might recede, leaving only salt to make its mark.

The cadmium wafted in through the open doors of the grain bay. It did not settle on the workers' hands, because they wore gloves. It didn't find their hair, which was covered by nets or white hats. It may have found its way onto the equipment in the open bay, such as tongs and stirrers. Two weeks later the chemist who managed the random sampling of the grain, dough, and finished product noted the trace of the element in batch 1104L/50. Subsequent batches didn't show the anomaly. The chemist put his findings into his monthly report. However, he was careful not to make a recommendation based on the spectrography. He labeled the cadmium a "trace unknown variant." Its appearance was within acceptable parameters, though privately, the chemist wondered what this country was coming to.

"Miss Vickers," he said, "How are you?" She looked up from her typewriter at his frame lodged across her door.

"No complaints," she said. The chemist laughed, and Miss Vickers coughed and said, "Excuse me." She was sick of their little joke. She had initiated it, and was now forced to repeat it for his amusement. She thought he was annoying, that he constantly prodded her to reveal if anyone had written in with a finding of a small tack in their cracker, or a burnt corner. In fact just that morning she had been deciding what to do with a long letter in tight, ill-schooled curls blaming the Rye Cracker Company for creating a cracker without any of the qualities that made food worth eating. The texture was bad, the flavor was appalling. Was the company trying to create soulless automatons who didn't have the energy to criticize the policies that were driving this country into a state of constant war? Were we being deprived of all pleasure with these unnatural health foods? Rye crackers tasted like cardboard, and what we put in our mouths decided the vibration and intensity of our thoughts.

The writer moved on to his dislike of his state's governor. He had seen dreadful scenes, the writer said, a couple beaten by the police on a Saturday night outside a grocery store for doing nothing. Just for being, the complainant wrote. These were Negro folks. He'd seen it also with Italians, treated like animals. Their apartments didn't have heat, but it was said they didn't need it, as they were fundamentally livestock. He'd seen a Negro boy knocked to the ground, kicked in the head, and handcuffed. Blood came out of his mouth onto the pavement. We shouldn't put up with this, he wrote. Are we blind? Are we deaf? We salute the flag for the freedom it represents, when actually we're living in a police state. What was the Rye Cracker Company doing to create such unfeeling, unthinking shells of human beings?

Miss Vickers didn't know what to do with this letter. She didn't have a formula for the response. She wondered if she should include it in the file for the lawyers. It might be considered a threat. Actually it was more of a castigation. She laid it in the file, then brought it back out from under its manila cover. The handwriting changed in size, and the lines were not evenly spaced. You could almost feel the tension in the hand that held the pen. "You poor nutball," she thought.

Struck

I KNEW THIS GUY WHEN I FIRST LIVED IN CHICAGO who visited the music store where I worked. The owner of the music store seemed to collect characters, including me. Not that I wasn't a mild-mannered and serious musical instrument saleswoman, but the owner told me I reminded him of Tippi Hedren, while vehemently criticizing my choice of clothes. I only later learned she was Alfred Hitchcock's favorite actress. If that tells you anything. The other clerk, Enrique, came to work after his days at one of the city's most prestigious magnet high schools. He was virtually homeless, staying on the couches of various friends, and probably undocumented. He was also a prostitute, or lived off gifts from boyfriends, but I didn't know any of that until he'd had to go to the emergency room after one of his dates turned violent. I knew this schoolboy Enrique only as a guitarist. Supposedly he was really good, but I never heard Enrique play more than a few phrases while he tuned up a guitar for a customer. I heard his friend Mark play once. Enrique invited him to the store. Mark had graduated from a private conservatory, but was now on the loose, with no prospects. Classical guitarists were not much in demand in the city or anywhere else, it seemed. An oboist or flutist could audition for an orchestra, and a pianist or harpist could get a gig on a cruise ship. But Mark's only employment was delivering pizzas. He had met Enrique somewhere, and he came into the store because Enrique invited him. He sat down on a chair by the counter and played us a piece that had been composed for him.

For a writer to describe music is very difficult. I could compare the notes to colors, write that he wafted blue and lavender scarves of sound by us, or say that the music felt peripheral, as if we were taking in only a side glance of it, while its whole momentous bulk hovered just beyond reach. I could describe Mark's bland, doughy face, his unmemorable features, and how while he was playing his instrument, his unremarkableness seemed designed not to distract from the historic agility of his hands. I could say the piece Mark played was like some other piece of music you might have heard, but I can't think what a good correlate would be. I can't even give it a genre, except contemporary classical guitar. This piece Mark's friend or teacher or unknown stranger had composed expressly for him called out of the instrument things I didn't know a guitar could do. This music had a silver mistiness, as there's nothing more beautiful than when the guitarist hits a harmonic—that is, rests his finger very lightly on the top of the string instead of pressing it down against the neck so the note plucked vibrates an octave above where it would otherwise be found. The composer, through this gifted guitarist Mark, conveyed a heavenly glistening, but he also dragged it down with some mysterious meanderings, the notes heading off into fetid alleys of an unknown city while sunset snaked its last sparks off the spires of tremendously influential corporate bank towers.

I learned at a later point, through what a well-informed friend had read on a reputable website, that the listener never hears music so much as remembers it. That's why when you buy a new CD or maybe stream for the first time an entire album by a jazz quintet you adore, at your first listen it's just a scramble. You don't even know if you like it. You're just trying to fix it onto what you already know. And then at the second listen, each note seems to have found its place. By the third time through, you can already hear the first chords of the next track as the last one is fading. This phenomenon creates a challenge for symphony orchestras that want to debut new and musically daring pieces. Even the most loyal symphony subscribers find themselves wondering when it will be over instead of remarking on the novel experience. The orchestra installs four trumpeters in four corners of the auditorium so that the sharp anthem will descend on the audience from all directions. The people squirm in their seats and remind themselves of the floor number and section of the garage where they parked their vehicle. The symphony subscribers can barely tolerate the debut, much less appreciate it. The ears long for familiarity, and in fact spend all their time trying to fit new sounds into old patterns.

As it is also with many books I've read and revered, I can't remember much about the piece Mark played, but I remember how it wrapped me up. I had no idea what I was hearing. The composition, and the way it took over this pudgy Mark and made a portal of him, opening us two music store clerks and our elderly boss into an alien cityscape where we were lost and terrified and tremendously grateful for the experience—all that lingers, but I couldn't say that the piece was Brazilian or in a major key or was eleven minutes long. Forgive my imprecision. You'll just have to take my word for it that listening to Mark play was a striking experience.

The music store owner made no attempt to hire Mark, though I imagine that's what Mark was angling for. My boss was a shrewd judge of character. Even so, Mark often stopped by to chat with Enrique. Without his guitar in his lap, he was an annoyingly dull person. After two or three conversations with him confronted me with his bland stare or his slightly spitting laugh, I ignored him. The most he got out of me was a nod to mark his entrance. Enrique and I talked about a lot of things, including how he took part in a protest against bilingual education. He felt his Spanish-language classes in elementary school had trapped him on a rung of low achievement he had been lucky to bust out of. Besides music, he was interested in the history of geodesic domes, and also in robotics and utopianism.

One Saturday morning Mark came into the store early. Enrique hadn't made it in yet, and the owner and I were inventorying an order of German metronomes. The store owner clearly didn't like Mark, but he read his bleak expression and offered him the chair next to the counter. Mark told us he had almost been killed. He'd been robbed at gunpoint while delivering pizza the night before. He took an order to an address that didn't look right to him, in an apartment block along the lake. As he stepped out of the car, two men jumped him, and one pressed a gun to the base of his skull. He felt the cold snout, in fact could feel it there still.

"I could have died," he said. "They got all my money."

While the owner considered that here was Mark, still alive, and that he had no one to tell his story to but Enrique's boss and colleague, I burst into tears. I wasn't thinking of Mark so much as the piece he had played us. No one else could play like that, and the piece itself was totally unique. It had been written just for him. If he had been shot in the head, that music would have vanished.

The store owner gestured toward the box of metronomes. There was nothing to cry about. Robberies like this happened all the time in the city. What did a pizza delivery guy expect? We had to finish our inventory in the next ten minutes.

Getting nothing from my boss, Mark gaped at my wet cheeks. His doggy eyes calculated that I might after all feel some compassion for him. "No, no," I stuttered, shaking my head and wiping my eyes. I read out the serial number of the next metronome. I said nothing about the remarkable composition he had played for us. I didn't say I still thought, no matter what happened, that Mark was a boring piece of shit. But given my moment of weakness, my behavior in the ensuing weeks would have to make my coldness toward Mark crushingly clear.

Later that summer I went to a free street concert, where the organizers had blocked off the intersection and rigged lights above a temporary bandstand. Four women in tall black hats wailed against a backdrop of clarinet and mandolin. I didn't go to the festival for the band in particular, but had showed up to meet some friends who lived nearby. We stood and talked, cupping each other's ears to be heard over the noise. Gradually, the forest shrieking of the four women outweighed whatever trivial things my friends and I had to discuss. We stopped talking and drew ourselves into the throng in front of the stage. After a few more steps forward, we could barely move, penned in by boy-like men in baseball caps and gloriously bare-armed young mothers. I looked up at the women on stage, giantesses in their fabulous headdresses.

I lowered my head, maybe checking on what sticky mess my sandal had dabbled into. At this slight motion, I entered a totally different soundscape. When I held my face toward my feet, the swirling sounds of the audience murmuring to each other and crackling their plastic beer cups filled my ears. With my head up, the four women unfurled their furious harmony. Angled down again, I made out a separate musical realm of infinite, undifferentiated hubbub. The crowd noises, vast and unorchestrated, hung underneath the composed music of the band. I only had to shift my chin to move from one level to the next. I hadn't noticed this interference or been bothered by it at any previous musical event. My ears had been doing the work all along, of skeining out the unwanted din. Now I was struck by what a rough base the women's music floated on.

Trusted Source

My sister Vicky lived for ten years with a man I never met. Our other sister Althea didn't meet Verne, either, and he appeared to my parents in person only once. After their initial clash, Verne spoke to my mother or father only through the closed door of his apartment, where Vicky may have been a kind of prisoner. My mother described standing in the hallway, filthy with spiderwebs, engaging in complicated negotiations about a holiday meal or my sister's mood meds. As Vicky had lost her license and was in any case terrified to drive, Verne would take her places, if he had time. "He's a blackmailer," my mother said, though without seeming too remorseful about it. Verne would agree to get Vicky to some needed appointment or happy occasion only if his gas was paid for in advance, and then some money offered for maintenance of his car, or if he was outright given a new set of tires. At least someone else had taken Vicky in and made her his problem, my mother seemed to say. She was pretty worn out by dealing with the middle child's travails, and maybe these sordid cash arrangements were actually easier than helping Vicky grow up and find a job. That would have been impossible.

Vicky's boyfriend was perpetually in court with the owners of his apartment complex. Though he paid his rent every month, Verne insisted on turning over the check on the fifth, and not the first. He claimed that legally he had a five-day grace period, and every month he took advantage of it. Meanwhile my parents kicked in Vicky's share of the rent, or what Verne had told Vicky to say was her half. "I'm not going to maintain her," he told them, though he also didn't let Vicky out of his sight. They went to the grocery store together, and to the video-rental store, and to a picnic table in Waltruther Park, where they liked to read in good weather. Verne allegedly did freelance graphic design and signage for a number of small businesses, working from his kitchen table. He took Vicky with him to make his drop-offs and pickups, but she stayed in the car when he went into the companies that hired him.

They'd taken a trip to North Carolina, where what might have been road rage led to Verne's arrest. He had Vicky call our mother, and she bailed him out. "Your daughter has no clean clothes," he told her another time, through the door. The washer-dryer in their unit had busted three weeks ago. He couldn't bring Vicky to an appointment unless he got six hundred dollars to replace the machines. "A dump like that has laundry in the basement, at best," Althea said. She couldn't believe our mother had fallen for this scheme, and she took over handling Vicky's finances.

When several years later Vicky called Althea to tell her Verne had died, Althea hung up on her. She hadn't meant to be cruel, she said, but she wasn't going to believe it without verification. Vicky hadn't known what Verne died of, she said, and she was stammering and incoherent. "Was it sudden?" Althea had asked, and Vicky seemed not to know what that meant. Althea was sure Verne was in the background, dictating Vicky's script. She wouldn't put it past Verne, she said, to have researched the cost of a funeral, with its okay, better, and best coffins, and chosen an exact amount the funeral home was demanding of poor Vicky to have him interred.

People will lie about anything, of course. The basis for the U.S. invasion of Iraq in 2003 rested on faked, faulty, and disproven intelligence. U.S. Defense Secretary Donald Rumsfeld claimed under oath in front of the Senate that he'd never seen reports that the documents that showed Iraq had bought so-called yellowcake uranium were faked. The forgery had been so obvious to the experts who looked at them that one wrote "even a simple Google search" would have been enough to expose them. However, since the defense secretary proclaimed under oath that he had no information about the forgery, this proved he did not have this information. Another version of this man might have seen the various unmatching fonts from the awkward cut-and-paste, may have read the notes that proclaimed simply and clearly that the document was not to be trusted. This version of the U.S. defense secretary shadowed the other one, like the Sunday self who relaxes on the couch versus the Monday self who knuckles down, or the past self who managed to plan ahead so the future self doesn't have to hustle. The defense secretary might have meant only that he had at one point existed as an entity that had not read the damning reports about the documents. He had been that person, he might have meant to say, who had lived in joyful ignorance. If he was now a person who had actually moved his eyes over an intelligence briefing that outlined the many obvious faults and irregularities in the yellowcake documents, he was still also in some sense that earlier version of himself who had not yet confronted this unpleasant evidence.

You couldn't sever this past version of himself from the present man speaking in front of you now, he may have wanted his listeners to conclude. Wasn't any man also his reflection, and his medical records, and the impression his voice on the phone had left with his secretary? How could any person be constituted as an essential entity, especially in an act as convoluted as reading? The reader always imagines a wholeness out of the partiality of words on the page, the defense secretary might have wanted to explain. The reader forms the whole, the conclusion, while the writer just lays down clues to it. And so if he said he had not seen the intelligence that posited that the yellowcake documents were an obvious forgery, in some sense he hadn't seen it, as he could not believe, no matter what the words said in so-called plain English, that what the U.S. defense secretary wanted to believe wasn't believable.

In this case, my sister Althea advised the rest of the family not to deal with Vicky until she sorted it out with the hospital where Vicky claimed that Verne had died. She called and asked their records office to fax her a death certificate. Althea was the kind of person who had a fax number, or at least no one to object if she received a personal fax while at work. The hospital representative told her it would take several weeks to complete the paperwork. A month later, the hospital still hadn't sent Althea a record of Verne's passing. She called again, and the sympathetic manager of the hospital's records office said that no death certificate had been issued as no one had claimed Verne's body. Verne had no next of kin. No relatives had surfaced. But he did die there, in the hospital? Althea persisted. Yes, he had. "Your sister," the records office manager told Althea, "is welcome to come claim the remains. We can release them to the funeral home of her choice."

In all this time of trying to determine whether Verne had in fact died, no one had said "My condolences" to Vicky. We hadn't asked how she was, but scoffed at the magnitude of this latest extortion attempt. We might have imagined that if Verne had passed away, then Vicky would be happy to have escaped this man who had such a tight leash on her. By the time the hospital records office had convinced Althea that Verne was dead, it was too late to start behaving like any of us were grieving. If I had patted Vicky on the arm or the shoulder, asked her how she was, and said "I'm sorry for your loss," the whole performance would have been painfully faked. "Why didn't you at least send a card?" Vicky asked me once.

I had no answer. But I continued to maintain that Vicky had gotten herself into this mess. She was the one who had taken up with an evil con artist, not me. I hadn't done anything wrong. It was her fault for getting entrapped by this person, who after all I had never met. Even Althea had never spoken to him. I had only heard about him. Verne was just a rumor, a conjecture. If Vicky was going to be heartbroken at having to go on without this figment, that was her business. I wasn't going to feel sorry for her. I wasn't sorry.

Umbrellas

A MAN NAMED T. S. CRAWFORD DEVOTED YEARS OF HIS LIFE to the study of umbrellas. A dentist with a thriving practice, he only got to speak on his specialty once a year. He formed a club with other umbrella enthusiasts. For the 1907 meeting, the enthusiasts gathered in a small side room in a rented hall in a Boston suburb far from the harbor. In the main room of the hall, mill workers had gathered to discuss conditions. The walls shook with their shouting. Three of the mill workers stood at the front and described a girl stooping to fix a bobbin on the loom, and the rollers taking her hair. They had watched as the machine bent her down and pulled her to it, inch by inch winding her toward its clacking gears. Luckily, her partner thrust a yardstick into the roller. The girl lost a six-inch strip of scalp, though her life was saved. What the mill workers wanted was an emergency switch to turn the things off, but they had been denied this safety feature.

In the smaller conference room in the back of the hall, the aficionados examined images of ancient umbrellas. Some were made of palm fronds, some of silk. Their holy colors had been white, gold, black, or red.

The enthusiasts agreed that the origins of the umbrella were entirely symbolic. Protection from rain was a late invention. At the beginning of civilization, the sky itself was understood as a woman's body arched over the earth, her toes and her hair touching at either end. The curve of her hip held the sun at noon. The umbrella spoke with its shape. It projected holiness and told a story of a benign universe. When the queen marched by under her sunshade, she was describing with this object her relationship to her people: I will shelter you.

"Ladies, ladies," shouted the mill owner's representative. It was the first time he'd come to a meeting. It was exactly as he suspected, a lot of emotion and very little reasonable discussion.

The umbrella club members shared their photographs and drawings of crowds in Burma. Bits of ancient manuscript laid out the price of silk, the process of making banana-leaf paper, the cost of an ordinary functional umbrella in various world economies. They looked at sliding ring mechanisms and Buddhist temple umbrellas shaped like upside-down wash buckets. The meeting was scheduled for ninety minutes, with tea afterward.

Next door, the women displayed their misshapen hands or badly healed wrists and told of their near misses. They described the bits of thread and cotton fuzz that floated through the mill air. They breathed in these fibers and coughed them out again on the dark, hot, noisy shop floor. They spat them off their lips and tongues hours after they had finished a shift.

The connoisseurs fell into their long argument, the two factions lined up with the plate of gingersnaps between them. The umbrella as shield from rain was not the same instrument as the holy shadow caster. Rains in the ancient world and every part of the East were torrential. No cloth dome could hold off the force of these vertical floods. People would have simply stayed home, or gotten wet. They could not have hurried up crooked alleys, their horizons narrowed by the dripping hem of the umbrella.

It was unjust how umbrellas, once replicating the divine sky, were now associated with gloom and drizzle. "It's a burden," one of the enthusiasts said. He had a small collection of prints showing various popes under umbrellas, and the others in the club believed he was actually Roman Catholic. "Your wife hands you an umbrella on a dreary morning, saying you might need it later. You'd feel so light without it, such a gambler. The sun might come out, but you have to be prepared for the worst. And you know she'll scold you if you come home wet. It's like you don't believe in anything. The umbrella shackles you with pessimism."

He was only trying to be provocative. The rest of the members didn't take him seriously. They looked at remains of yellow fringe pressed between plates of glass. Their newest member relayed a synopsis of an essay on hunting dogs. None of them knew why. It turned out he was thinking of breeding his spaniel bitch, and his tale had little to do with squirrels or raccoons or hunting horns or Beethoven, and not at all with umbrellas, though when he had started out, he had implied that he was responding to what was left of a pattern on the material in front of them. Various tartans and calico checks had regional significance, he had said. They watched his red lips, seeming so bare under his mustache, as he went on about his two sons and how his wife couldn't get them to eat vegetables. The umbrella enthusiasts were all past the moment when they had thought he was making a long detour that would nevertheless return to the subject under study, and therefore widen the orbit of the umbrella's influence. An umbrella formed an entire world around a person, especially on a dark evening when the only light was reflected from streetlamps out of puddles. This world could have anything in it, including baying hounds and women's songs. But that wasn't what he was talking about.

"It's a simple thing," the mill workers shouted. The mill's representative could hardly get to the question and answer period. The women seemed to already know all the answers. They were in fact fixated on this safety switch. They didn't have the skill or the discipline to do the math for the cost of implementation. It was far more than the price of the gizmos themselves, it was the production process interruption, and the possibility of further shutdowns at any silly whim. They would be the ones to pay for that, if the mill wasn't profitable. They couldn't think that far ahead. Did they want to lose their jobs? The mill's representative looked out into the sea of buns and braids, the scornful eyebrows, the open mouths. They had to bind their hair tighter, he thought. It was in most cases their most beautiful feature, but it didn't accord well with the machines.

One of the mill workers, looking for a back door to the yard, wandered into the scholars' meeting. "Umbrellas?" she said. The newest member offered her a gingersnap. The rest of them looked away. One of them might have thought how an umbrella furled and held tight under its narrow strap and snap was like a widow in a dress. No breasts, but waist and hips, and the flaring hem around the ankles. Out in the street, when it began to sprinkle, a hand pressed the mechanism and the widow disappeared. She was now something else entirely, an even array of struts.

If they had asked the mill worker, she might have told them about the mildewed tub in the orphans' home where the umbrellas suffocated, face down in their own mess. The club men had their own memories of desecration, the umbrella abandoned beneath a barstool or in the corner of a restaurant, the closet at the theater that held all the lost scarves, gloves, and umbrellas. An usher or a patron caught out might borrow one of these castoffs. The goddess's body passed hand to hand, only temporary, each new user leaving it without a thought behind a chair or on a window ledge. Many people didn't even bother to repair their umbrellas. Broken ones accumulated in closets under stairs. New ones poked out of displays at corner cigar stands, unnoticed until it stormed, and then it was too late.

The mill workers filed into the night. They were sure they had gotten somewhere. It had been worth it. They breathed in the mist rising from the bricked street. The corners and intersections separated the crowd, combing out its density. The umbrella enthusiasts walked together to the streetcar, now talking about taxes and the bad habits of their managers, brothers-in-law, or secretaries. They lugged the boxes of their collected goods, while their own favorite umbrellas swung from their forearms. A few of the mill workers sat at the back of the car, still furious but also laughing. However, the umbrella club couldn't identify them anymore as part of the group that had rented the bigger part of the hall. The mill workers had a unified look to them, but no insignia. Out in the world, they were just women.

The enthusiasts had not talked at all about the sound of rain hitting an umbrella, or how a person's cuffs got wet, but their thighs stayed dry. If you were walking with a person under one umbrella, each got wet on the outer half, left arm and left leg soaked, and your partner the mirror image. They had not brought up the sensation of walking along in your own darkness, and then noticing that the sun had come out. The brightness after the umbrella went down was a widening, a lack of limit. For some this was a happy moment, but for others, fearful. The streetcar too was like an umbrella, and so was a house, or an auditorium. A day could be faced with bare barbarity, or dimmed down and circumscribed by the umbrella's skin. The best time for umbrellas was midafternoon. The primitive inventors of the umbrella could not have known what a crowd of businessmen would look like, seen from the third floor of an office overlooking the main artery of a commercial district. The goddess herself, now withdrawn from the earth and looking down from a safe distance, might remark at a misty boulevard filled with black circles. What a beautiful sight, this momentary shielding of the heads and all their wishes and quarrels. Seen from above, the umbrellas simplified the writhing humans into a floating geometry. Their metal spikes and caps glinted. Water ran down their ribs as the tide of city people tilted and jostled. The collection of umbrellas lofted down the narrow sidewalks like flower petals, uniform. It might have looked from this vantage like the umbrellas comported themselves by themselves, no fierce hands gripping their sticks.

Voorhees

WHILE VISITING SOME OLD FRIENDS IN CHICAGO last weekend, I stepped into a museum to get out of the rain. An artist had several galleries to himself or herself, someone with a name with a strange doubling of vowels, like Saar or Adaams or Hooff. I can't remember except that it was like Voorhees, but not Voorhees. Anyway this artist created a limited vocabulary of shapes—something like a comb; a rectangle with a wedge cut out of it; two triangles oddly fused; a blocky hourglass—and made paintings, sculptures, and other objects out of them. Maybe eleven or twenty-one shapes that she laid on top of and next to each other in a palette of dark brown, dark green, and pink, these colors like a 1930s hotel lobby's palm-tree wallpaper, tropical and harmonious.

Everywhere I looked, these shapes looked back. One piece of carved wood sat in a high niche, ten feet above me, as if watching the gallery visitors from a safe remove. The sculpture's same shape, now flat, figured in the large painting on the wall below it. There the shape floated atop the other shapes, severed from the attentiveness of its sculptural iteration. On another wall, two smaller paintings also held a combination of the shapes, aligned differently. Each symbol in Voorhees's vocabulary could mysteriously change place, and go from heavy to light, anchoring to escaping.

In the center of the room stood a desk, clearly handmade by the artist, a sculpture of a desk. The artist's collection of shapes had cooperated in forming a smooth writing surface. They found their fullest expression in the desk legs and chair back. Despite some unique properties, Voorhees's desk looked very much like my mother's desk, the one she gave to me. I'm writing on it at this moment. As a child I loved her desk because it had cubbyholes and two tiny drawers, now stuffed with my own receipts and letters, the warranty for my broken wristwatch, and passwords unwisely scribbled onto half index cards. On Voorhees's desk lay two books, or sculptures of books, closed, of the same size, bound in gray linen. One of Voorhees's symbols was stamped across the front cover of the top book. The symbol also presumably marked the identical book below it.

The second gallery held a mock bookshelf—a bookshelf created by the artist to look like a bookshelf, which she may have altered from a commercial bookshelf, or from one she had found on the street in Buenos Aires. Slim volumes of gray linen showed their spines, each imprinted with one of the symbols in pink. Although the books were identical in size, shape and covering, they had been shoved or flung or placed into the bookshelf as if the action of placing had taken place at different times, with different intents, as if the identical books were in fact each separate entities.

I took it as a threat almost—out of these few repeated shapes a whole library arose. Over there, in the first gallery, the woman writing at the desk. Around the corner, in the second gallery, the woman reading. Or a proposed person might be able to write. Able to read. Voorhees dealt in possibility, I thought, making her fairly contained world wild with ungovernable prospects: where there were no human representations in her artwork, no faces, hands, butts, or throats, there still lingered the impression of busy masterminds churning out and consuming meaningful tchotchkes.

All the time I actually lived in Chicago, thirty years ago, my friends and I only went to museums on the occasional free Tuesday. Sometimes in extreme heat, we paid to experience the air conditioning. Where a huge park now celebrates the edge of the lake, we used to go for picnics in wasteland. As we walked out to a promising spot, we scared up pheasants nesting in brambles between the rails of abandoned train tracks. From our blanket we watched the light change across the profiles of the glass buildings of the Loop. Only a hundred yards away, men and women in business clothes hustled between sightseers stepping off tour buses. This stretch of land seemed utterly forgotten, hemmed between the restless lake and the grandeur of Michigan Avenue.

Another place we liked to go for fun was Tire Island. On a small spit of land in the middle of the Chicago River, someone or many people had piled thousands of used tires. The water swirled around the island, thick with foam from industrial effluents. While the water made its rapid, messy passage around the island, the tires waited indifferently in their stacks. Created for rolling down highways, they now lay on their sides, immobile, like ancient horses out to pasture. Nothing bothered them. Even as the tallest towers listed, sloppily composed, they never altered. My friends and I hiked to this desolate spot not too far from the neighborhood where we'd settled, honing our keen observational powers and our sense of apartness from striving. We didn't enjoy working toward goals, but liked to mosey around.

In those days my friends and I were very poor. We entertained ourselves by wandering and noticing. One afternoon, I went to a sliding-scale health clinic with my daughter and wrote down my income in the space provided on the intake sheet. This number came through on my patient chart. The doctor looked at me with horrified concern, as if this annual before-tax figure was an ominous medical test result for a condition he couldn't cure. I myself wasn't troubled by the number until I saw his expression. I thought sliding-scale clinics existed exactly for people like me and my baby. I should be treated, without judgment, for my ailment. The doctor seemed to think the fault for whatever illness I had was mine. I was stupid for living with it, and for not railing against it. Such ignorance he couldn't treat. He would do his best for my current physical symptom, his astonished face said, but it wouldn't be much. Not nearly enough.

Waiting

It doesn't happen so much anymore, the gap between the thought and the action, the writing the letter and then finding the address, followed by a long period of forgetting and then remembering to come up with an envelope, then a stamp, and then to finally write the address on the envelope carefully centered left to right and up and down. Even after all this preparation, the letter didn't have to go anywhere. The stamped and sealed envelope sat on the table, or was folded into a notebook. It took a long time to decide to drop it into the mailbox, to watch it slide irretrievably into the gullet. Then waiting for the reply—it could take a year. It's a mark of the modern, not to have to wait. The people of today have the conquering spirit, the certitude, the rightness, the lack of ambling or loitering. But somewhere there still must be doubt. Waiting and doubt.

Waiting is watching for the appropriate time to do something, though we may never know if the right time actually comes. Waiting is also a low-level city worker planting herself on the corner where the bus stops. When I lived in Chicago we used to wait hours for the Ashland Avenue bus to come after midnight. It sometimes got off schedule by a good ninety minutes at three or four in the morning. The sight of it finally nearing, still a quarter mile away, caused an immense rush, the deliverance, at last, after so much tedious expectation.

The waiter of course waits on your desires to be made plain, though often the tables are turned, and you feel helpless, waiting for the waiter to get back with the bread. Making someone else wait is a show of power, and to be able to outwait the other is a victory.

All this is obvious. I can't wait long enough to have enough thoughts to finish writing something called "Waiting." Imagine a pill you can take, like a probiotic, that makes you smell wonderful to yourself, from the inside. Every exhale looses a little bit of fennel and calm, a feeling of pure goodness, which is now how you experience yourself. Picture constantly feeling like a little girl being given a cookie, the kind of little girl everyone wants to kiss on her cheek, and she wriggles away and won't let anyone touch her because she's so precious to herself. Not everyone experiences that, even for a moment, and any of us who once did can't hold onto it. It doesn't accord so well with adulthood. Imagine that people taking these pills, which are not very expensive but not too many people know about them, have a slight advantage over everyone else in simple things: being called out of turn at the bakery; the Jiffy Lube guy giving them an upgrade to the coupon special even when they don't have the coupon. Like being pretty and young, but it's internal. Then everyone else finds out and gets mad. "I hate those fucking patchouli ghouls," they say, "so self-satisfied."

Great harms are visited on these confident, pill-prepped winners. They're knocked down in the street, pushed onto the subway tracks, threatened with broken bottles, cursed and spat on. "You think you're so special!" their assailants shout. Even conked with billy clubs and placed in choke holds, these pharmaceutically enhanced souls think to themselves, "I know I deserve better."

Waste

It seems a tragedy that there's so much waste, not only the buried piles of mattresses and diapers, rotten railroad ties, and crumpled soda bottles, but the gusts of elm seedlings and the river of potential humans squirted out to no purpose in a morning jerk-off. Billions that could have become trees, become souls, are simply wasted. Yet if everything is part of the same totality, then there is no waste, simply material designated as waste. That's not the same thing.

Waste results from an unequal distribution, an inability to smooth the graph of consumption and destruction. The horizon at sunset, when the lake is totally flat and calm, promises for once an even division, water and sky. The conditions we live under always require too much, and then too little. Only by moving through these disasters over a long period of time can we gather, over the course of a life, exactly what was needed.

Indulging in wastefulness creates a pleasure that veers toward the perverse. A diner sits with her artichoke, scraping off the soft, flavorful bit, the rest of the leaf too fibrous and tough to be consumed. The leaves pile up—in fact she needs two plates, a small plate for the whole artichoke, steadily diminishing in its pool of released steam, and a much bigger platter where she flings the used leaves. Similarly with mussels, only the small, defenseless creature is eaten in its wine sauce, and its much larger outer carapace is tossed out. The fastidious would like to collect the used mussel shells from the backs of bistros and bleach them, grind them, and strew them on garden paths. But there's no time for that. The sea creatures' unwanted exteriors stink in black barrels until they make it to the landfill.

A restaurant in Connecticut serves only moose lips, in a recipe the chef perfected after he'd left his last restaurant in a drunken fury. He offers the softest, most tender cut of meat imaginable, slivers of fat that dissolve on the diner's tongue like ghosts in daylight. Outside, along the staff parking lot, the departing patrons glimpse a tangled heap of moose carcasses. The hulk of unused corpses is almost as big as a barn. At most the antlers have been taken for trophies. Maybe the chef sells the legs to a dog-food maker. While reversing past this ghastly heap, the diners try to recall their joy at the first taste of moose lip, slipping away even as it announced itself. Now a nauseating burp recalls the continued actuality of the meal inside them. And what are you but a bunch of junk, the chef would like his diners to wonder. He wants them to struggle to find within themselves a tiny lump of gooey mercy.

A woman went to visit her old college roommate Marie in Baltimore. She took her out to dinner for her fortieth birthday, thinking that at this point, the prickly Marie had no friends or any family who would care to make a fuss over her even once every ten years. She emailed her boyfriend a plaintive note: the visit had been going fine, had been pleasant, and then Marie spent twenty minutes ragging on an acquaintance who had put her mother into hospice long before it was warranted and was in Costa Rica during her mother's final moments. Her old roommate's vituperative outburst, the woman wrote to her boyfriend, was enough to ruin the day they'd spent poking around antique stores, and the sweet card she'd picked out, and the flowers she'd bought. Marie takes everything so personally, she wrote. Like it's for her to decide how other people's mothers die.

During a low time last winter, a few months after Vicky's death, I asked some of my writer friends to give me their discarded words. I thought I could create something out of the ones they had backspaced over, as my attempts to move forward with my own had come to a dead stop. I wrote appeals in email and Messenger to people I admired, and asked for words they had deleted. I'll take good care of them, I promised.

My friend Chris said he did very little revision, and anything he didn't use, he guarded carefully. His wife Annie, however, sent me a whole paragraph, set in a font that crossed it out, as if you were reading it through a fence. Stefan sent me a sad half phrase, utterly insignificant, and exactly what I was hoping for. I gathered several more from my generous friends, and copied these wasted bits of others' prose into a document. I waited for them to transform into something new and beautiful. I imagined a collage-like essay made from these unrelated phrases, a quilt of glimmers, stutters of unformed beginnings.

I checked every morning, but the wasted sentences refused to knit together without more instruction from me. They sat on their page, and nothing happened. The borrowed phrases didn't combine, ferment, or even decay. I was going to write about waste, I had told these word donors. I thought about Vicky's apartment, and how much better it had looked once Althea and I cleared all her shit out of it. We picked up sloganed coffee mugs and a little display of dolls on her side table, thinking some of this stuff had significance. But really, none of it did. I tried on a pair of her winter boots. They actually fit me. But in the end I decided that the way the heels sloped down a tiny bit on the outer sides, from Vicky's slightly bowlegged walk, spoiled them for me.

Anything Althea and I came across that seemed to be of better quality, not quite yet all the way broken or dented or soiled, turned out to be something Althea or my mother had bought for her. We drove these to Goodwill: Vicky's radio, the boots, a down parka, a desk lamp, and a few more presentable wooden chairs and a table. All the rest we threw into black plastic lawn-and-leaf bags, which we lugged out to the dumpster behind the building. The way the bags banged against my legs made me slightly queasy, hearing the thump and crunch coming from the mix of hard and soft items knocking together. As soon as I released the bags into the bin, I felt fine.

The two of us carried Vicky's couch, its foam shedding through tears in the blue-flowered upholstery, down the back steps. We dropped it beside the dumpster. Someone in the neighborhood might have taken it, if they were that desperate for something to sprawl on. Or this couch on which Vicky had lounged until she was too weak to hold her paperback got picked up by the city waste-disposal crew, the one that drives the big machine with the claw on the front to hoist bulky, unwanted items.

When at last the apartment was empty and Althea had vacuumed, it looked almost decent. The rooms appeared a little bigger with no furniture to impede the sightline between door and window. The absence of Vicky's tangled blankets, her stacks of novels, and the dolls and postcards she had collected, seemed much better than the presence of these traces of the person who had touched and used them. The unadorned walls seemed to prove that Althea and I had done our duty, like good sisters, clearing the place out. Our mother wasn't in any fit state to pitch in.

We hadn't remembered to take any pictures, and the only ones we have now are the ones Althea texted to the apartment manager to show her the emptied cabinets. "Here is the potential our sister wrecked with her crap," Althea's texts might have said. "Please let the next tenant have their chance at making a mess out of it." But Althea, being much more pragmatic than me, just sent the shots, documenting the stains in the shower stall and the loose closet doors. Even so, we didn't expect to get Vicky's deposit back. Althea had paid it in the first place, but she let it go. Though Althea is very frugal, she said it was easier that way, not to have to fight over what damage Vicky did or didn't cause to the premises. Just living in a place wears it down and makes it dirty, she said. Apartment managers should realize that more than anyone. But they pretend otherwise.

The other day I stumbled on this collection of real estate shots on my phone while I was scrolling through looking for something else. At first I didn't recognize the rectangles of beige carpet and the precisely framed images of opened drawers. Who put these here? I thought. My privacy had been invaded. Next to photos of my kids, all grown, at an outdoor restaurant with their cousins, someone had inserted these oddly bland images of unoccupied space.

Then it hit me that it was Vicky's place, our only record of it. Althea must have shared them in a folder with some family shots. Here were my and Althea's kids. Here was the featureless flooring of Vicky's last rental. During the moment when mystery passed into recognition, I felt something foam up inside me. It felt almost like kindness, a kind of softening, or the very beginning of understanding.

Xyz

Twice in the past few weeks I passed a helicopter hovering about shoulder height off the ground. I was driving by the air field on the way to the store, my routine trip. I wondered why the thing didn't land or go higher. It stayed nearly upright, not even making much noise, the rotors a blur, but their wind hardly making an impression on the shorn grass below. The airstrip looks more like a soccer field, the tawdry domesticity of open space set up against two-story apartment buildings on one edge, a row of muffler and brake shops on the street perpendicular. The pilot must need to practice, I thought. They sent him way to the edge of the field and told him, just hold it a few feet up. The pilot might be involved in mountain rescue someday, holding steady while others lifted stretchers or maneuvered tarped bundles of supplies below. "What we want you to do, Alex," his superior shouted, "is just hover, okay? Keep it steady." Experience must have taught the soldiers that keeping the craft in the air right above the ground was more difficult than sending it swooping away. Going through the air was the good part. Anyone could manage it. Doing barely anything, staying at eye level, nothing exhilarating, took nerves and stamina. Resolve.

After she died, I wanted to write about my sister, but the sister in this book is not exactly her. Her name wasn't Vicky. That's a name no one in our family would ever have gotten stuck with. Victoria, possibly. Vicky doesn't ring right, and that's why I chose it. Most of what I've described of Vicky comes from my real sister's actual words and interactions. I've quoted from one of her poems, though the time and circumstances of her poetry's composition isn't quite what I've said it was. When her longtime boyfriend died, my family did indeed believe it was a hoax, designed to extort money. Her remark about Elton John remains with me. Of course there's much more incident that I haven't included, and much that I've altered for my own convenience, mostly in the details of persons and places surrounding my sister. Where we lived, and who did what, and complications that I've streamlined. But I can say that it's true that shortly after she died, her shade came and sat on my bed.

"What are you doing here?" I said, scolding her as always. It was the same outraged tone I had used with her throughout her life. What a fuck-up she was, what a wreck. Such an idiot, she didn't even know that when you died, you stayed dead. Incredible, I thought. Only Vicky could screw up death. Such a failure. Althea—who isn't really called Althea, nothing like it—will never believe this, I thought, when I tell her.

Acknowledgments

The inspiration for this book came from Dave Buchen, the artist whose work graces the cover of *Afterlife*. Dave is a Puerto Rico–based artist with a letterpress in San Juan. Years ago he commissioned me to contribute to a multivolume work he planned to illustrate, print, and sell in installments to subscribers or investors, to be called *Encyclopedia Deiknumena*. I forgot what the title meant as soon as he explained it to me, but I believe it has something to do with staring at something for a period of three days. He asked me to write the encyclopedia entry on encyclopedias, knowing how much that would suit me. He even offered to pay me an extravagant sum. But not only did he not find my submission particularly apt, the whole project foundered: the investors not showing up, Hurricane Maria altering Dave's outlook on how he made a living, and other projects pushing *Encyclopedia Deiknumena* into the realm of the abandoned. I persisted, expanding on my first entry and eventually asking Dave if he minded if I wrote the whole encyclopedia myself. Gradually this work parted ways with *Encyclopedia Deiknumena* and became an encyclopedic meditation on the loss of my sister. I am profoundly grateful to Dave for giving me the initial spark, and for encouraging me to do what I wanted with his encyclopedia idea.

My investigation into the diffusion of cadmium over Minneapolis in 1950 is in debt to Nicholson Baker's *Baseless*. Thank you to Gabriel Blackwell, editor of *The Rupture*, for including "Voorhees" in that journal's final issue, to Sven Birkerts and William Pierce at *AGNI* and Bradford Morrow at *Conjunctions* for publishing excerpts, to Cara Hoffman at the *Anarchist Review of Books* for publishing "Cults," and to Robert Lopez, Derek White and Garielle Lutz for selecting "Birds in Art," "Cadmium," and "David Copperfield" for the twentieth-anniversary edition of *Sleepingfish*. Thank you to David Wells and Edgewood College for providing me with a retreat at the Painted Forest. Thank you to the writer who was the model for Quinn in the entry "Fallujah," whose story and experience of reading it to his class I have borrowed—I haven't been able to find you to ask permission, and I hope you don't mind. Thanks to Sarah Blackman at FC2 for encouraging me to submit the manuscript, and to the whole FC2 board and the University of Alabama/FC2 staff for carrying on the work of publishing books like this. For my small gang of writer friends in Madison, especially Sara Greenslit and Krista Eastman, I'm grateful every day. I'm also deeply thankful for my family for being okay with my writing stories of our sister that don't belong to me alone, but to all of us who grew up with her and continued along with her as a troubled, sometimes amusing, sometimes tragic adult.

www.ingramcontent.com/pod-product-compliance
Lightning Source LLC
LaVergne TN
LVHW011837060526
838200LV00053B/4068